START FROM SCRATCHES

MORGANA BEST

Start from Scratches
A Paranormal Women's Fiction Cozy Mystery
MenoPaws Mysteries Book 3
Copyright © 2021 by Morgana Best
All rights reserved.
ISBN 9781922595317

Cover: Enchanted Ink

GLOSSARY

*S*ome Australian spellings and expressions are entirely different from US spellings and expressions. Below are just a few examples.

It would take an entire book to list all the differences.

For example, people often think "How are you going?" (instead of "How are you doing?") is an error, but it's normal and correct for Aussies!

The author has used Australian spelling in this series. Here are a few examples: *Mum* instead of the US spelling *Mom*, *neighbour* instead of the US spelling *neighbor*, *fulfil* instead of *fulfill*, *realise* instead of the US spelling *realize*. It is *Ms*, *Mr* and *Mrs* in Australia, not *Ms.*, *Mr.* and *Mrs.*; *defence* not *defense; judgement* not *judgment; cosy* and not *cozy; 1930s* not *1930's; offence* not *offense; centre* not *center; towards* not *toward; jewellery* not *jewelry; favour* not *favor; mould* not *mold; two storey house* not *two story house; practise* (verb) not *practice* (verb); *odour* not *odor; smelt* not *smelled; travelling* not *traveling; liquorice* not *licorice; cheque not check; leant* not *leaned; have concussion* not *have a concussion; anti clockwise* not *counterclockwise; go to hospital* not *go to the hospital; sceptic* not *skeptic; aluminium* not *aluminum; learnt* not *learned*. We have *fancy dress* parties not *costume* parties. We don't say *gotten*. We say *car crash* (or *accident*) not *car wreck*. We say *a herb* not *an herb* as we pronounce the 'h.'

The above are just a few examples.

It's not just different words; Aussies sometimes use different expressions in sentence structure. We might *eat a curry* not *eat curry*. We might say *in the main street* not *on the main street*. Someone might be *going well* instead of *doing well*. We might say *without drawing breath* not *without drawing a breath*.

These are just some of the differences.

Please note that these are not mistakes or typos, but correct, normal Aussie spelling, terms, and syntax.

AUSTRALIAN SLANG AND TERMS

Benchtops - counter tops (kitchen)

Big Smoke - a city

Blighter - infuriating or good-for-nothing person

Blimey! - an expression of surprise

Bloke - a man (usually used in nice sense, "a good bloke")

Blue (noun) - an argument ("to have a blue")

Bluestone - copper sulphate (copper sulfate in US spelling)

Bluo - a blue laundry additive, an optical brightener

Boot (car) - trunk (car)

Bonnet (car) - hood (car)

Bore - a drilled water well

Budgie smugglers (variant: budgy smugglers) - named after the Aussie native bird, the budgerigar. A slang term for brief and tight-fitting men's swimwear

Bugger! - as an expression of surprise, not a swear word

Bugger - as in "the poor bugger" - refers to an unfortunate person (not a swear word)

Bunging it on - faking something, pretending

Bush telegraph - the grapevine, the way news spreads by word of mouth in the country

Car park - parking lot

Cark it - die

Chooks - chickens

Come good - turn out okay

Copper, cop - police officer

Coot - silly or annoying person

Cream bun - a sweet bread roll with copious amounts of cream, plus jam (= jelly in US) in the centre

Crook - 1. "Go crook (on someone)" - to berate them. 2. (someone is) crook - (someone is) ill. 3. Crook (noun) - a criminal

Demister (in car) - defroster

Drongo - an idiot

Dunny - an outhouse, a toilet, often ramshackle

Fair crack of the whip - a request to be fair, reasonable, just

Flannelette (fabric) - cotton, wool, or synthetic fabric, one side of which has a soft finish.

Flat out like a lizard drinking water - very busy

Galah - an idiot

Garbage - trash

G'day - Hello

Give a lift (to someone) - give a ride (to someone)

Goosebumps - goose pimples

Gumboots - rubber boots, wellingtons

Knickers - women's underwear

Laundry (referring to the room) - laundry room

Lamingtons - iconic Aussie cakes, square, sponge, chocolate-dipped, and coated with desiccated coconut. Some have a layer of cream and strawberry jam (= jelly in US) between the two halves.

Lift - elevator

Like a stunned mullet - very surprised

Mad as a cut snake - either insane or very angry

Mallee bull (as fit as, as mad as) - angry and/or fit, robust, super strong.

Miles - while Australians have kilometres these days, it is common to use expressions such as, "The road stretched for miles," "It was miles away."

Moleskins - woven heavy cotton fabric with suede-like finish, commonly used as working wear, or as town clothes

Mow (grass / lawn) - cut (grass / lawn)

Neenish tarts - Aussie tart. Pastry base. Filling is based on sweetened condensed milk mixture or mock cream. Some have layer of raspberry jam (jam = jelly in US). Topping is in two equal halves: icing (= frosting in US), usually chocolate on one side, and either lemon or pink on the other.

Pub - The pub at the south of a small town is often referred to as the 'bottom pub' and the pub at the north end of town, the 'top pub.' The size of a small town is often judged by the number of pubs - i.e. "It's a three pub town."

Red cattle dog - (variant: blue cattle dog usually known as a 'blue dog') - referring to the breed of Australian Cattle Dog. However, a 'red dog' is usually a red kelpie (another breed of dog)

Shoot through - leave

Shout (a drink) - to buy a drink for someone

Skull (a drink) - drink a whole drink without stopping

Stone the crows! - an expression of surprise

Takeaway (food) - Take Out (food)

Toilet - also refers to the room if it is separate from the bathroom

Torch - flashlight

Tuck in (to food) - to eat food hungrily

Ute / Utility - pickup truck

Vegemite - Australian food spread, thick, dark brown

Wardrobe - closet

Windscreen - windshield

Indigenous References

Bush tucker - food that occurs in the Australian
bush

Koori - the original inhabitants/traditional
custodians of the land of Australia in NSW. *Murri*
are the people just to the north. White European
culture often uses the term, *Aboriginal people.*

Detective Cole is missing. Nell has a gut feline all
is not well, but JenniFur, Edison, Daphne, and
Delilah do not seem concerned.
When a man is found murdered, Nell and her
friends discover all is not cat and dried.
Soon they are chasing their tails. Will they find the
detective before it's too late? One thing is for sure,
it all starts from scratches.

I said good morning to the cat, and the cat said good morning to me. That was one of the strange things about JenniFur. She said good morning, while most cats said, "Do not greet me. You are not worthy of a hello. Feed me. Feed me or suffer my wrath."

Also, she said good morning in English.

"I want food," she said. A magical cat was still a cat, after all. Her manners only stretched so far.

"I *am* feeding you," I replied, opening a can of tuna.

"If you do not feed me this very second, I will vomit on the carpet." JenniFur ran in front of my slippers.

"You know, you would get fed a lot faster if

you didn't try to trip me up every time I walked towards your bowl."

"How can I trust you won't forget to feed me?" JenniFur replied. She head-butted my calf.

"I feed you every day," I muttered, emptying the can into her bowl.

I stood, tossed the can into the recycling bin, and glanced in the mirror. I looked a mess. My hair was in the type of curlers my grandmother had worn every night for seventy years. I didn't mean the curlers looked the same; they were her exact curlers. I'd inherited them while my cousin, the favourite, inherited her home, furniture, and savings.

"Feed me," JenniFur said.

I looked down at her. "I literally just fed you?"

"I don't recall," JenniFur said, "I feel as though I haven't been fed in seventeen years."

"You were fed five seconds ago," I said, even though I knew there was no point in arguing with her.

JenniFur did not reply. Instead, she vomited on the rug.

I groaned. "Great! Why can't you throw up outside?"

"It's cold outside," JenniFur said. "I would like my breakfast now."

I cleaned up while JenniFur tried to trip me up. Then I fed her again, because I wanted two seconds of peace and quiet to remove the curlers from my hair. I didn't get the chance in the end, because there was a knock on my door.

I lived above my bookstore called *A Likely Story*. It was a cozy, quaint little apartment deep on Wild Lime Mountain. The man who ran the bookstore, Edison, was a small, wizard like individual who sometimes knocked on my door with coffee and crumpets. After the stress of JenniFur, I was looking forward to the caffeine.

I opened the door. "Edison, that's so sweet."

But it wasn't Edison. It was Detective Caspian Cole. Caspian was ridiculously handsome. Seriously, no man had any business being that dashing. I scrunched up my nose, trying to keep out his cologne, which was warm and spicey and inviting.

"Check out the buns," JenniFur said. If she was a person, I figured she would have wolf whistled.

"That is wildly inappropriate," I said. For a moment, I had forgotten that Caspian had no idea I could speak to JenniFur. I was the only one who could hear her thoughts.

"No," JenniFur said, she was purring now. "The finger buns."

It turns out she was not talking about Caspian's bottom, but the bread covered in icing and sprinkles.

"Why have you brought those?" I said, thinking the only place those buns would go would be straight to my buns.

"A bribe." Caspian looked flustered.

"I'm listening," I replied.

"Oh, are you ever," JenniFur said.

I ignored her.

"My niece is in town for a while."

"I didn't know you had any siblings." I stepped to the side to let Caspian into the apartment.

"Neither did I," he replied, "until three years ago. It turns out I have a half-brother who is fifteen years younger than I am. We're not at all close, but he's asked me to look after his daughter, Harriet, for a few weeks. She's my niece."

"Yes," I replied. "I'm aware how families work, Caspian. Is everything okay?"

"Oh, yes. My brother's away on business. I

don't know the first thing about kids, Nell." Caspian ran a hand through his hair.

"You're a homicide detective. I would think taking care of a kid would be easy for you."

"What do they eat?" he asked.

"How old is she?"

"I have no idea. She's so small. Tiny. A baby, really. With these beady little eyes, like a shark."

"Where is she now?"

"At home," he said.

"You left a baby at home, alone?"

"No, Edison's watching her. I called him before I popped over. He's watching her while I speak to you."

"Okay. Well, do you have anything at home for her?"

"Like what?"

"Oh, Caspian, like formula. Teethers."

He paled. "Oh no!"

"That's no drama. We'll stop by the shops on the way to your house, okay?"

"My brother's going to kill me," Caspian said.

"He does have nice buns too," JenniFur said as I closed the apartment door. The day had already descended into madness, and it was not yet nine o'clock.

We bought formula, a teething toy, a rattle, three bibs, three onesies, and a breast pump. We hadn't meant to buy the breast pump, only Caspian had shoved anything from the baby section into the cart, and I hadn't noticed until we packed the car. It was one awkward situation on the drive over to his house, trying to explain how a breast pump worked. Men really were another species.

Edison hurried out of Caspian's home when we parked outside on the road. "Thank goodness you're here," he exclaimed. "She's a monster. A monster!"

He hurried to his car and drove away.

"How bad could a little baby be?" I thought as I looked towards the house.

It turns out Caspian's niece was not a baby but a *teenager*. She stood on the porch, arms folded, glaring down at us. Her hair was brown but with two chunky strips of bleach at the front, and her fingers were decorated with the kind of plastic rings my daughter had loved when she was Harriet's age.

"You said she was tiny," I muttered to Caspian.

"She is tiny. Look at her."

"I'm Nell," I called out to Harriet.

"Whatever."

"You gave me the impression she was a baby," I hissed.

"I said she was tiny?"

I exhaled. "Then why did we buy baby stuff?"

Caspian shrugged. "I followed your lead. You're the one who knows about children."

Ignoring Caspian, I walked over to the house. "Are you looking forward to spending the next few weeks with your uncle?" I asked sweetly.

"Please. This town is so boring. Wild Lime Mountain? Gross. I could have been with Maddie at the beach."

"But does Maddie have teethers?" Caspian said, unloading everything we had bought from the supermarket.

"This stuff is for babies," Harriet said. She rolled her eyes. "I'm not a baby, Uncle Caspian. I'm thirteen."

"A terrible age," he said.

"What's this old lady doing here anyway?"

"I'm not an old lady!" I exclaimed. "I'm fifty-something. I might not even be halfway through my life."

Harriet groaned. "I don't want to learn how to knit."

"And I don't want to teach you how to knit," I replied.

Harriet narrowed her eyes. "Do you know Kung Fu?"

"Yep," I said. "I'm a ninja."

"Really?" She brightened.

"No, of course not."

To my surprise, Harriet laughed. "Okay. Sorry. But Maddie's grandmother is a Kung Fu instructor. Isn't that cool?"

"That's lovely. Look, I'm sorry you're stuck on the mountain for a few weeks, but I own a bookstore. You're welcome to stop by anytime you feel bored."

"I love books," Harriet said. I could tell she was warming up to me, even though I didn't teach Kung Fu. "Do you sell coffee?"

"You're not allowed to have coffee," Caspian said. "You're thirteen."

Harriet rolled her eyes. "Whatever, Uncle Caspian. What's your Internet password?"

Caspian told her, and Harriet disappeared into the house. Teenagers can only waste so much energy on adults before they needed to bail. I understood. I was a teenager once myself many moons ago. I didn't plan on telling Harriet that, though. Everybody her age seemed to think that fifty-year-olds had always been fifty, that we were born into an advanced age, and that the sands of time would never touch their naive little heads. If only that were true.

"You've got your hands full with that one, Caspian," I said affectionately. I liked spirited girls. The world too often tried to crush that spirit out of them.

"That's why I bribed you with finger buns. I need help," he said.

"Well, for starters, feed her pizza. Kids love pizza. And pasta. Make it extra cheesy. I'd also recommend giving her an allowance if her brother didn't leave her any money."

"He didn't."

"With an allowance, she can buy books and snacks when you're out."

"What if she spends the money on cocaine?"

"Oh, my goodness, Caspian. There's no cocaine on Wild Lime Mountain. You're a detective. You should know that. Besides, just because she's a teenager, doesn't mean she's into drugs. She likes books. She said so herself."

"Pizza. Pasta. Books. Okay. I think I can do all that." Caspian frowned. "Hey, Nell, were you talking to your cat before?"

"No! What. Maybe. Hmm?"

"It sounded like you were talking to someone before I knocked, only there was no one else in your apartment."

"I'm a crazy cat lady," I said. "What can I say?"

Caspian nodded. "Thanks for your help."

"Thanks for the finger buns. I'd better get moving."

"Sure," he replied. "Do you need to take the rollers out of your hair."

"What rollers?" I said. I reached up to touch my hair, only to remember that I was still wearing my grandmother's rollers. "Oh no!" I was absolutely mortified. My ears burnt with embarrassment.

I looked down at my feet. I was still wearing my slippers. In fact, I was still wearing my pyjamas too. They were not even cute pyjamas, but long johns with a butt flap. For a horrid moment, I thought the flap might have fallen open, but when I reach around to check, it was still buttoned close. Well, that was something.

"Why did you let me leave the house looking like this, Caspian?"

"I don't know anything about fashion," he said.

"This is not fashion. This is pyjamas."

"I think you look fine."

"No woman wants to look fine, Caspian. Why is it that men think it is acceptable to tell women they look fine? We want to look glamorous, breathtaking. We want to look unhinged. Anything but fine!"

"You look unhinged," Caspian said. He seemed puzzled.

"Thank you," I replied.

Harriet burst through the front door. "Can you people keep it down, please? Adults are so annoying. Why don't you both chew loudly and sneeze while you're having your little lovers' tiff!"

With that, Harriet slammed the door, leaving us on the porch.

Caspian's face flushed red. He opened the door for me. "You go inside." I opened my mouth to protest, but he held up one hand to forestall me. "You don't need to speak with Harriet. Sit in the living, room and I'll fetch the nice bottle of wine I just bought. I left it in the car. It's the least I can do. First, I'll give Harriet some money."

I smiled and walked inside. To my relief, Harriet was nowhere to be seen. I walked into the living room and sat on a comfortable couch. I hadn't been in Caspian's house before. It was masculine, the large Chesterfield couch on which I was sitting was upholstered in dark blue fabric, and there was a dark brown leather Chesterfield opposite. It looked much younger and in far better condition than the leather Chesterfield in the reading room in my bookshop and the even older one in my living room.

I stared at the fire. They were real flames, and it took me a few moments to realise it was one of those fires that looked like a real wood fire. That was certainly a plus. I did love open fires, but I didn't like the venomous snakes and deadly spiders that came with firewood, although thankfully the deadly Funnel Web spider wasn't usually found this far north.

I shuddered and looked at the doorway. Caspian was certainly taking his time. I crossed to the window and looked out. His car was still parked on the street, and the door was open. There was no sign of Caspian.

That was strange. I walked to the front door and opened it. I walked outside and looked in his car. He wasn't sitting there, speaking on his phone. I was turning around to go when I noticed what I thought was blood on the ground.

I gasped, but on closer inspection, it was only red wine.

That's when I saw the broken glass. The wine bottle was shattered, its pieces glinting in the early morning sun.

Where was Caspian?

CHAPTER 2

*M*y heart was beating out of my chest. I hurried back inside. "Harriet!" I called. "Harriet!"

She appeared, a petulant look on her face. "What?"

"Have you seen your uncle?"

She narrowed her eyes. "Are you mad? Of course, I have! I saw him a few moments ago when he gave me his credit card."

"I didn't mean then," I said tersely. "He said he was going to the car to fetch a bottle of wine, but there's no sign of him, and the wine bottle is broken."

"Maybe he cut himself and came inside to treat it," she offered.

I pushed past her. "Caspian! Caspian!" I called repeatedly, but there was no response.

"Harriet," I said urgently. "Hurry! Search the house for your uncle."

To my surprise, the girl did as I asked. I went back outside and looked up and down the street.

There was no sign of Caspian. My mind ran through all the possibilities. Had there been a police emergency and somebody had collected him? No, because he would have had time to come back inside and tell me. I couldn't think of a possible single logical explanation for Caspian going missing like that. I walked down the side of the house and looked in the garage. He wasn't there.

I made my way back to the front door. Harriet rushed through it. "He's not in the house!" she said. "Has he been kidnapped?"

"Who would want to kidnap him?" I said, rubbing my forehead vigorously.

"You can tell me the truth. I'm not a child," she snapped.

"I don't have a clue what's happened to him. Maybe he *has* been kidnapped." My reply seemed to placate her somewhat.

"Should we call the police?"

I nodded. "That's a good idea." I hurried back into the living room and fetched my phone from my handbag. I asked to be put through to Detective Sam Stevens. As soon as he answered, I said, "Hi, this is Nell Darling. I'm at Detective Cole's house. He wanted me to meet his niece. He went outside to his car to fetch a bottle of wine, but he didn't come back. I went to the car, but the car door was open, and the bottle of wine was smashed on the road. There's no sign of him."

I walked out to the car and looked at the glass on the road as I was speaking.

Detective Stevens took a while to respond. "I'm not sure why you called me."

"But he's missing, don't you see? He vanished into thin air. I think he's been kidnapped."

"Kidnapped?" Stevens's tone was incredulous.

"Yes, kidnapped," I said firmly. "Maybe it's something to do with a case you're working on. He disappeared about twenty minutes ago. His niece and I have searched the house, and he's nowhere to be seen."

"Have you called him?"

I planted my palm on my forehead. Why hadn't I thought of that? "No. I'll do that right now." Without another word, I hung up on the detective and called Caspian's number.

At once, I heard a phone ringing. The sound seemed to be coming from under the car. I leaned down. There, under the car, was a phone. I got down on my knees on the hard road, wishing I had a cushion to kneel on, and tried to reach for his phone. It was a little too far away. I struggled back to my feet and called the detective back.

"Please take this seriously," I said. "His phone is under his car. I really think something has happened to him."

"If he doesn't turn up in a couple of hours, call me back," Stevens said.

I pushed on, considerably annoyed. "But why would his phone be under the car? Look, you're a detective, so it should be obvious to you that something's happened to him. He went to the car to fetch a bottle of wine, and he was coming back inside at once. The bottle is smashed, and his phone is under the car. Don't they say the first few hours are the most important in the case of a kidnapping?"

Stevens sighed again. "All right. I'll drive up to Wild Lime Mountain and check it out. Will you stay at his house until I arrive?"

I told him that I would.

I turned around and almost walked into Harriet. "What's happening?" she asked.

"Your uncle's partner, Detective Stevens, is coming up here now," I said.

She nodded. "I heard. Do you want me to try to reach Uncle Caspian's phone?"

I shook my head. "No, best to leave it there and let the police process it. This is the scene of a crime."

Harriet's bottom lip quivered, so I quickly added, "Try not to worry. Your uncle's very clever, and he can look after himself."

She narrowed her eyes again. "I suppose it's good that there's no blood splattered around," she said.

My breath caught in my throat. I hadn't thought of that. "Err, yes, yes," I sputtered. "We had better get back inside and wait for Detective Stevens."

With a shrug, she walked back along the garden path, with me following behind her. She opened the door and disappeared. I walked into the living room. I paced up and down, looking out the window at intervals in case Caspian returned. It was going to take Detective Stevens at least half an hour to drive up the mountain, and that was if he left as soon as I called. The waiting made me nervous.

My phone rang, and I jumped. For a moment I hoped it was Caspian but realised nanoseconds later that his phone was under his car. I looked at the caller ID: Edison.

"Edison," I began, and was about to tell him what had happened when he interrupted me.

"Where are you?"

"I'm still at Detective Cole's house," I said. "But Edison, he's vanished! He ducked outside for a minute, and the bottle of wine is smashed, and his phone's under his car. I think he's been kidnapped!" My voice rose to a high pitch.

"I'm sure he's fine." Edison's tone was dismissive. "But Nell, something terrible has happened."

"Terrible?" I repeated. "What do you mean?"

"I'll have to tell you in person," Edison said and then quickly added, "It's nothing to do with your family or anything like that. Can you come back to the bookshop straightaway?"

"No, I can't. I have to wait for Detective Stevens. He's coming to investigate Detective Cole's disappearance."

"I'm sure he's fine," Edison said again. "A more pressing matter has arisen."

"Edison, please tell me what's going on. I can't take the suspense."

"All right, Emerson Mortcombe is dead."

"Dead?" I echoed. "Oh, that's absolutely terrible! What happened to him?"

"He was murdered, of course," Edison said. "But they say it's natural circumstances."

I scratched my head. "When did this happen? Was Caspian called to the scene? Or Detective Stevens?"

Edison didn't answer for a moment, and I imagined him shaking his head. "No, the police haven't been called. The doctor insists it was natural circumstances, but Emerson Mortcombe was murdered."

"How do you know?"

"That's what I need to tell you in person. I can't trust this sort of information over the phone."

"Could this have something to do with Detective Cole's disappearance?"

"No, he's probably just popped to the shops, or he's talking to a neighbour," Edison said, once more dismissively.

I opened my mouth to say he couldn't have driven to the shops as his car was still there, but Edison was still talking. "But Nell, be very careful. Come back to the shop as soon as you can and don't take any detours. You could be in terrible danger."

CHAPTER 3

*D*etective Sam Stevens took an hour to arrive. At least, it was an hour before I saw him. I just happened to look out of the window and saw him crouched down, looking under Caspian's car. I had no idea how long he'd been there.

I hurried outside, but Harriet beat me to it. "Where is my uncle?" she demanded to know.

Detective Stevens jumped, banged his head under the car, said a few rude words, and then straightened up. "Who are you?"

"I'm Harriet. Uncle Caspian is my uncle." She rolled her eyes, possibly as she had said the word *uncle* twice in a row. Who would know?

"He's not here."

Harriet rolled her eyes again. I took over the conversation before she said something I would regret. "Something's happened to him," I said, in the firmest tone I could muster. "Like I told you earlier, he said he was just popping out to the car to fetch a bottle of wine. When he didn't come back, I went outside and found the wine bottle smashed all over the road, and his phone was under the car. I suspect he's been kidnapped. At any rate, it's clearly foul play."

This time, Detective Stevens seemed to take my suggestion more seriously. He scratched his head. "It does seem strange. And he said he was only going out to the car?"

I nodded. "Yes. He said he'd be right back."

"And there's no blood," Harriet said.

The detective scratched his head again.

"Are you working on any particular case that would cause somebody to kidnap him?" I asked. I held up both hands, palms outwards. "I know you can't tell me the details, but something's happened to him."

"We're not working on anything that could lead to a kidnapping." The detective bit his lip. "Did you touch anything?"

"No," I said. "Are you going to process this as a crime scene?"

The detective looked doubtful. It was a while before he responded. "I'll call the forensics team just to be on the safe side." He looked at Harriet. "But I'm sure there's no need to worry."

Harriet planted both hands firmly on her hips. "Look, Sherlock, it's obvious that there *is* a need to worry. My uncle has vanished into thin air." She waved her arms expansively.

The detective turned to me. "I'll let you know if I find out anything. Meanwhile, if he contacts you, call me at once." He looked at Harriet. "And you too."

"Of course. Harriet, you'll have to stay with me until your uncle turns up."

Harriet crossed her arms over her chest and her expression took on a darkened aspect. "I'm not a child!"

I thought fast. "Of course not, but if your uncle has been kidnapped, you might be next, and I'm possibly in danger as well, given that I'm a friend of his. We'll need to protect each other. Collect your things and come and stay with me at the bookstore."

Harriet's expression relaxed a little, although she was still petulant. "All right, if I have to."

She turned on her heel and stormed inside the house. I followed her along the path and waited in the hallway for her to reappear. She did so presently, with a backpack and a large striped shopping bag. When she saw me looking at the shopping bag, she said, "PlayStation and Nintendo Switch."

"I see," I said, although I didn't really. "We should leave a note for your uncle. Do you have a pen and a sheet of paper?"

Harriet dropped her backpack on the floor unceremoniously, lowered her shopping bag with far greater care, and then stormed out of the room, only to return moments later with pen and paper. She thrust them at me. "Here."

"Thanks." I walked over to the coffee table and left a note telling Caspian where we were, although I was certain he wouldn't come back—not without being rescued from someone or something.

When I reached the front door again, I asked, "We'll need to lock up the place. Could you lock the back door and all the windows?"

"Can't you lock the windows?"

I nodded. "Of course." I hurried around, checking all the windows and was back at the front door before Harriet. "You have a key to the front door?" I asked her.

She produced a key and waved it in front of my face.

"Okay then, let's lock up and go."

The short trip to my bookstore was silent. Harriet stared fixedly out of the window. Tension emanated from her in waves. It was most uncomfortable, to say the least. I hoped she wouldn't be any trouble.

As it was a Monday, the bookstore was closed. On the mountain, given that it was a tourist town, most storekeepers took their weekends on Monday and Tuesday, the quiet days. I did sometimes open on those days as well, but I had shut today.

When I opened the door, Edison jumped in front of me. "Thank goodness you're here!" he said.

He gasped when he saw Harriet behind me and then at once smiled. "Hello."

"Detective Cole is missing," I told him, "so Harriet is staying here until he turns up."

Edison nodded absently. "I'm sure he'll show

up." He looked around the room wildly, no doubt wondering how he could tell me what was going on now that Harriet was here.

"Caspian is missing?" said a voice from under the couch. JenniFur stalked out and looked Harriet up and down. "She's obviously a hardened criminal. Do you think she murdered him?"

"Of course not," I said. "This is his niece."

"Are you talking to the cat?"

I spun around. "Yes, yes," I stammered.

Harriet hurried over to JenniFur. "What a pretty cat!" she exclaimed. "A pretty fat ginger cat. I love cats." She picked JenniFur up and clutched her to her chest. JenniFur purred loudly.

"What a nice girl," JenniFur said. "I liked her the minute I laid eyes on her."

"Harriet, can you call your father? I want to tell him what's happened."

Harriet grunted, called her father, and thrust her phone at me.

Thankfully, he answered. I explained the situation as quickly as I could. He was happy for Harriet to stay with me, which I thought a little odd given that he didn't know me from a bar of soap. "Please call me if you hear from your brother," I concluded.

"Edison, why don't you come with me to the kitchen and we'll see if we can find some ice cream for Harriet," I said. To Harriet, I added, "You can plug your PlayStation and um, your other thing into the TV if they'll work on it."

Harriet, still clutching JenniFur, hurried over to the TV and looked behind it. "Yes, this is fine. I thought you might have one of those ancient TVs." She put JenniFur down gently and rummaged through her shopping bag. I gave Edison a significant look and hurried towards the kitchen.

When we were safely in the kitchen, I asked in lowered tones, "What's all this about?"

Edison leaned forward. "Emerson Mortcombe was murdered."

"Yes, you told me that. But what makes you think he was murdered when the doctor said his death wasn't due to suspicious circumstances?"

"Because he was killed with *Old Magic*."

As soon as Edison said the words, a chill descended upon the room as if winter had suddenly struck. Frosty fingers reached for my throat. I shook the fanciful notion away. "What's

Old Magic, and how do you know it killed Emerson?" I asked.

Edison looked behind him before responding. "The Seelie used Old Magic in the early days, but then it was forbidden. In the wrong hands, it's horribly dangerous."

"So, is it like very evil magic or something?" I asked.

Edison shook his head. "There's no such thing as evil magic. Magic is neither good nor bad. It's like energy. Energy can be used for cooking and heating, but it can also be used to kill somebody. It's the same with magic. It's the user that makes magic good or bad, not the magic itself."

I waved one hand at him in dismissal. "Yes, yes, I know all that, but then what's all the fuss about this Old Magic?"

Edison shuddered. "Because it has the potential to be dangerous to the extreme. As far as I know, it hasn't been used in centuries. It's elemental."

"But what makes you think Emerson was killed by Old Magic?"

Edison sighed long and hard. "I suppose I should start at the beginning." He pulled out a chair and sat on it.

I crossed to the fridge and selected a tub of salted caramel ice cream. I scooped some out into a large bowl and stuck a spoon in the top. When I walked into the living room, Harriet was playing a game, and JenniFur was sitting beside her, purring loudly. I placed the ice cream bowl in front of her.

"Thanks," she grunted, staring fixedly at the screen. She didn't notice that JenniFur ate some of the ice cream.

I hurried back to the kitchen. "I don't think she'll be going anywhere soon," I said. "Now, Edison, you've got to tell me everything."

Edison wiped a hand over his brow, and his face turned white. "Emerson borrowed a book from the bookstore."

I held up one hand. "Wait, I thought Prudence was the only one who borrowed books from us."

Edison pinched the bridge of his nose. "This was no ordinary book, Nell. This was a book from the secret room."

I jumped to my feet, nearly knocking my chair over, before remembering Harriet was in the next room. I sat down with a thud. "The secret room!" I hissed. "Is that the secret room behind a door that vanishes?"

Edison nodded.

I pushed on. "You told me it didn't exist!" I shot him my best glare.

"I'm sorry about that, Nell," he said in reasoned tones, "but I didn't want to tell you until you had settled in. It's all too much information, you see."

"Go on," I said through clenched teeth. "Exactly what is in this secret room?"

"Ancient books, grimoires, and other arcane volumes," Edison said. "To prevent them from any possibility of being stolen, we keep the room concealed with spells. Even JenniFur didn't know about it."

A clap of thunder punctuated his remarks. Where had that storm come from? "I hope the power stays on," I said, given that the TV was all that was keeping Harriet occupied.

"And Emerson borrowed a book. It was a book on Old Magic."

I thought it over. "Then maybe he accidentally killed himself with Old Magic," I said. "You yourself said nobody these days should wield it."

Edison shook his head. "He borrowed it because there have been rumours that an ancient power, an ancient organisation, is regrouping." He lowered his voice and whispered, "The Anvil and Reed."

"I've never heard of it. But that doesn't mean Emerson didn't accidentally blow himself up, so to speak," I said.

Edison shook his head once more. "The book is missing."

I thought it over. "You don't think he hid it somewhere for safekeeping?"

"He was clutching a piece of a page of it when he died. And what's more, there was a terrible sense of magic in the air, Old Magic." Edison's hands trembled.

I nodded. I knew Edison was a Hierophant and sensitive to magic outbursts.

Edison was still speaking. "I felt it and hurried over to his house, but it was too late."

"And you called a doctor?"

Edison held up both hands, palms to the ceiling. "Of course. Emerson was dead. I knew he'd been murdered, but the doctor said he'd had a heart attack. I could hardly call the police and say he'd been murdered with Old Magic, could I?"

"No, of course not." I clutched my forehead

with both hands. "This must have something to do with Detective Cole's disappearance."

Edison appeared puzzled. "How could it? He doesn't have anything to do with Old Magic. But Nell, don't you know what this means?"

"No?" I was entirely perplexed.

"Whoever took the book from Emerson Mortcombe and murdered him might think we have other such books at the bookstore. The murderer might come here looking for them. And that means our lives are at risk."

CHAPTER 4

The knock on the door startled me. Edison and I exchanged glances. I stood up and made to move towards the door, but he put a restraining hand on my arm. "What if it's the murderer?"

"Murderers don't knock, surely?"

Edison dismissed my notion with a shake of his head. "I'm sure many do."

The knock came again. "I have to answer it."

Edison and I walked to the door. I opened it a crack and peeked around it. "Daphne and Delilah," I said to Edison.

I opened it, and Delilah tumbled into the room, followed by Daphne.

"A terrible thing, poor Emerson murdered!"

Delilah shrieked. "And next we'll all be murdered in our beds!"

Before I could tell her that Harriet was there, Harriet appeared by my side. "We're all going to be murdered?" She clutched JenniFur more tightly to her.

"Of course not, dear," Daphne said. "My sister is nuts." She turned to address me. "And who is that youthful person?" She looked Harriet up and down with a clear look of distaste.

Clearly, it was mutual. "Is this your great-great-great grandmother?" Harriet asked me. "And her twin sister?"

Daphne gasped, so I hurried to say, "This is Daphne and her twin sister, Delilah."

"It's Ms Dimples to you," Daphne said coldly. "And who might you be?"

"I might be lots of people," Harriet said, "but I'm actually Harriet. Detective Cole is my uncle, and he's been kidnapped."

"I knew it!" Delilah waved her arms around like a helicopter's blades, dislodging her tinfoil hat. She picked it up and put it back firmly on her head. "I knew the aliens were likely to come back and kidnap somebody else." She turned to me.

"But don't worry, Nell. The aliens will return him to you."

Harriet stared at Delilah with obvious interest. "Aliens kidnapped my uncle? There's no such thing as aliens."

Delilah tut-tutted. "Clearly, you've been brainwashed. Here, take my hat and wear it for a while. That will help." She removed her tinfoil hat and shoved it hard onto Harriet's head.

I thought Harriet would have a tantrum, but she didn't seem to mind. "Thanks," she said, although her tone held doubt.

"Honestly, Delilah, you're scaring the poor child."

"I'm not a child," Harriet snapped. She narrowed her eyes at Daphne. "And why are we going to be murdered?"

"Of course, we are not all going to be murdered," Daphne said. "Delilah has a good imagination. She *does* believe in aliens kidnapping people, you see."

Harriet had apparently lost interest in the conversation because she grunted and went back to the TV.

Edison nodded towards the kitchen, and we

followed him back in there. "Who is that dreadful child?" Daphne hissed at me.

"I quite like her," Delilah said.

"You would!" Daphne snapped. "She reminds me of you as a child."

Delilah beamed, although I knew it wasn't a compliment.

"She's Detective Cole's niece," I told them. "He's gone missing."

Delilah's mouth fell open. "Missing?"

I nodded and repeated the story for what seemed to the millionth time that day.

"There's probably quite a normal explanation, and he will turn up at any time," Daphne said in bored tones.

"But who would have kidnapped him?" Delilah asked me.

"Who said he was kidnapped?"

Delilah rounded on her sister. "Didn't you listen? Nell said he was kidnapped."

"No, she didn't! And how would Nell know?" To me, Daphne said, "Did you see anybody kidnap him?"

"No, but…" I began, but she interrupted me.

"See! Nobody knows what's happened to him."

"But he was kidnapped on the same day that Emerson Mortcombe was murdered," I pointed out. "There has to be a connection."

"They can't possibly be a connection," Daphne said. Edison nodded vigorously in support.

Delilah and I exchanged glances.

Edison, "We have to increase the protection for this bookstore and your apartment, Nell."

"We don't have to move into Nell's apartment and camp here like the last time we were all in mortal danger, surely?" Delilah asked.

"No, I'm thinking Nell and Edison should stay with us," Daphne said. "It's the bookstore that's the target."

Everybody looked at me expectantly.

I shrugged. "That's very kind of you, but I will see how I feel when it gets closer to night time. At the moment, I feel I'll be safe, but it's easy to feel safe in broad daylight."

Another clap of thunder made me jump. "Well, maybe not broad daylight, but it's easy to be brave on the morning of even a stormy day." I realised I was rambling, but I was worried about Caspian, and I was also worried upset that Emerson had been murdered.

49

I hadn't known Emerson well. I had only seen him once or twice. He had reminded me of Edison, a tall, slender man with a shock of white hair and a bushy white beard, looking for all the world like Dumbledore or Gandalf, although he looked considerably older than either of them.

"I've explained to Nell about the secret room," Edison admitted.

I gasped. "The two of you knew about it?"

The sisters nodded. Delilah had the grace to blush. Daphne's face remained impassive.

"Is the secret room sufficiently protected?" Daphne asked Edison.

"Yes, of course," he said. "I'm concerned that the murderer or murderers will break in here and try to find other secret volumes."

I cleared my throat. When I had everybody's attention, I asked, "Exactly *what* was in the book that was stolen from Emerson?"

"I told you," Edison said. "It was about Old Magic."

I shook my head. "Yes, I know that. What I meant was, was it a history of Old Magic, or was it a grimoire, a book of spells?"

Once more, the familiar chill descended upon the room. "It is a book of Old Magic spells,"

Edison said. "Luckily, it was written in the language of the Tuatha De Danann. There's nobody who can translate that."

"Clearly, the murderer thought he would be able to translate it or he wouldn't have stolen it," I pointed out.

"The murderer must know something we don't," Delilah offered.

Daphne rolled her eyes. "Really? You think?" She snorted rudely. "We need to increase the protection around the bookstore, and since the police can't help solve a murder by Old Magic, then we need to figure out who the murderer is as soon as possible."

Something occurred to me. "If nobody knows how to use Old Magic anymore, and it's only in the book that Emerson borrowed from the secret room which was subsequently stolen from him, then how did somebody manage to kill him with Old Magic?"

"It's the organisation I told you about," Edison said in hushed tones. "An ancient organisation that's regrouping. They must have had access to Old Magic, although I assumed it had all died out. They obviously knew enough to murder Emerson, though."

"Edison knows that because he is a Hierophant," Delilah told me.

"Nell knows that," Daphne snapped. "And what about the child?" She turned her attention to me.

"She's staying with me until Detective Cole turns up," I said.

"No, I mean, does she know about the Seelie? Does she know her uncle is a Seelie of the Night Court?"

My hand flew to my mouth. "I don't know! I don't have a clue, to be honest. She's the daughter of Caspian's half-brother. Caspian only discovered he had a half-brother a few years ago."

"Then we will have to tread carefully." Daphne nodded slowly as she spoke. "We can't have the girl knowing anything about the Seelie. We will have to assume she doesn't already know."

Edison pulled a notepad from his right pocket and a pen from his left pocket. "Let's go through the basics. Either the murderer was somebody known to Emerson, or it was somebody who was not known to Emerson."

Daphne pursed her lips. "That sounds like something Delilah would say."

Delilah smiled widely. "Thanks!"

Daphne scowled at her and then scowled at Edison.

"I'm stating the obvious, *obviously*," Edison said, looking none too pleased. "If you would allow me to finish. As we have no way of investigating people who were *not* known to Emerson, then I suggest we investigate those who *were* known to him."

"That makes sense, I suppose." Daphne's tone was begrudging.

"I doubt Edison would allow just anybody into the house when he had the book in his possession," Edison added. "Of course, he could have been beguiled by Old Magic. All that aside, I've been thinking it over, and three people spring to mind." He stabbed his pen on the page.

Daphne piped up. "I suspect his cleaning lady, Nora Beckett," Daphne said. "A dreadful woman. If you ask me, she's the murderer. I've never liked that woman. She's rude, and she eats with her mouth open."

Edison opened his mouth to speak, but I forestalled him. "If any of these suspects have used Old Magic, wouldn't you pick it up?" I asked him.

"Only at the time," Edison said.

"The Old Magic wouldn't cling to them like a cloud of perfume or something?"

"Actually, perfume is a good analogy," Edison explained. "If somebody used Old Magic, it would be similar to using perfume. It would be as though someone used a lot of perfume, but if they went home and washed it off their clothes and showered, then no traces of that perfume would remain. It's the same as Old Magic. If I happened across a person just after they had used it, I would know, but it would wear off if they didn't use it continually."

I nodded.

Edison pushed on. "Indeed, Emerson's cleaning lady is the top of my list. There's also Logan Tate, the doctor who attended."

I was confused, and I said so. "But didn't you call him to the scene?"

"Yes, but he was a drinking friend of the victim's. They went to the pub together every Friday night."

"And who else is there?" Delilah asked.

"Emerson's football buddy, Algerone Riverty."

I found the conversation troubling. "Weren't all these people friends of his? Would someone pretend to be his friend just so they could get their hands on a rare book?"

"It wasn't just any book," Daphne said. "It was a rare book of Old Magic spells. One of a kind."

I shook my head. "That wasn't what I meant. How would they know Emerson was going to borrow the book?"

Edison tapped his chin. "Emerson has been borrowing books from the secret room for years. He's been trying to translate the old volumes. Maybe somebody found out." He tapped himself on the head. "I mean, obviously somebody found out."

Daphne agreed with him. To me, she said, "Emerson knew ancient languages: Akkadian, Sumerian, Hittite, Middle Egyptian hieroglyphics. He was a university lecturer and retired to Wild Lime Mountain many years ago. At the University of Sydney many, many years ago, he was taught ancient languages by Athanasius Pryor Treweek, who certified Ventris and Chadwick's decipherment of Linear B as correct."

I was doing my best not to look blank. "I think this all has something to do with Detective Cole's disappearance," I said again.

"He'll turn up at any minute," Daphne said. "But for now, we have more important things on our mind. Emerson was murdered, and the murderer took the book. Whoever did it is likely to try to find more books on Old Magic."

I gasped. "Do you mean there are more?"

"Yes, we have more but none anywhere near as detailed as the one that was taken," Edison said. "Of course, the perpetrator would not know that."

Delilah stood up. "Which is precisely why we could all be murdered!"

Harriet stepped into the room. "I was listening at the door. I heard everything you said."

CHAPTER 5

*M*y blood ran cold. "Exactly what did you hear?" I asked her.

"That you think we're all going to be murdered."

"Anything else?" Daphne asked.

Harriet pouted at her. "Isn't that enough? Shouldn't we get weapons or something?"

I rubbed my hand over my forehead. Thankfully, Harriet hadn't heard about the secret room, or if she had, she wasn't letting on. I figured it was the former, given that Harriet didn't seem to be the type of person to keep her thoughts to herself. She was nothing if not forthright.

Daphne gestured to her sister. "Delilah is as

mad as a hatter, to be honest with you. She has an overactive imagination. Can't you see how she's dressed?"

All eyes turned to Delilah. I had been so caught up in Caspian's disappearance and Emerson's murder that I hadn't noticed what Delilah was wearing. It wasn't really anything out of the ordinary to somebody who was used to seeing her, but to Harriet, I imagined it was quite a shock.

Delilah was wearing fluorescent lime green tights, with fluorescent pink, fur-lined boots halfway up her calves. A long silver shirt hung to just above her knees, and over it was a bright red, wide plastic belt. The effect was enough to give somebody a migraine. Plastic bracelets stretched from wrist to elbow on her right arm, and blue evil eye bracelets stretched from wrist to elbow on her left arm. Huge rings adorned all her fingers.

"I like your look," Harriet said.

"Thank you." Delilah beamed from ear to ear. "Do you feel much better wearing that hat?"

Harriet simply shrugged and handed the hat back to her. Delilah wasted no time putting it on.

"So, we're not going to get murdered?"

"Of course not," I said firmly. "I'll have to

think about a bed for you in the spare room. There was one here when I moved in, but I gave it away. I use that room now for all my books, my personal books, that is."

"They have air beds, and you can get a little electric motor for them so they inflate very quickly," Edison told me.

I clasped my hands with relief. "Do they sell them up here on the mountain?"

Edison's face fell. "No, but they sell them down on the coast."

I didn't want to do a long round-trip to the coast with Caspian missing and a murderer on the loose.

"I really think you should stay with us tonight," Daphne said. "And then, if it's safe, I can lend you a good air bed for the rest of Harriet's stay."

Harriet narrowed her eyes. "Do you think we'll be murdered if we stay here?"

"Of course not," Daphne said, although her tone wasn't altogether convincing. "Nell comes for dinner once a week, and I always urge her to stay for a fun slumber party afterwards. As you're both coming to dinner tonight, I wanted you both to stay."

"You can have my spare room," Delilah said. "It has a nice big TV in it."

"Did you buy the TV in the last decade?" Harriet asked.

"Yes, only a few months ago. It's twice as big as Nell's TV."

Harriet brightened considerably. "Okay, that sounds like a good idea. Um, don't you both live in the same house?"

I figured she was asking because Delilah had referred to the spare room as hers. "You'll understand when you see the house," I told her.

To Daphne, I said, "Then that's settled. Thanks so much for the offer of dinner and a sleepover."

Harriet walked back into the living room. I tapped Edison on the shoulder. "I want to see that secret room, and right now," I hissed.

Edison frowned. "What if Harriet sees us?"

"Delilah and Daphne can keep an eye on her," I said. "And where's JenniFur? She should have warned me that Harriet was listening in to our conversation."

Daphne did not look pleased in the least that she had to mind Harriet, but she pursed her lips, shot me a glare, and walked into the living room.

I grabbed Edison by the elbow, and I guided him into the bookstore. "I need to see what this is all about," I said.

He sighed long and hard. "All right, but don't be cross with me, Nell. It was for your own good."

"All will be forgiven as soon as I see what's in there," I told him. I made a shooing motion with my hands. "Go along now. No time like the present."

We stopped alongside a wall to my right. It looked like just any other wall in the bookstore. Edison muttered an incantation and waved the fingers of his right hand. A door appeared.

I gasped. "How come I saw it once or twice when it was hidden behind an incantation?"

Edison shrugged. "Possibly as you're a Bookmarker," he said. "You only saw it on and off, didn't you?"

I nodded. "One minute it was there, and the next minute it wasn't."

Edison did another incantation and opened the door.

I stepped inside. I hadn't known what I expected to see, but this room resembled an ancient library or maybe an office from Hogwarts. My attention was caught by the only source of natural illumination, a grilled window high on the far wall.

Edison followed my gaze "That's hidden behind an incantation too," he said. "From the outside, it looks like a solid wall."

Edison switched on a light, and the room was at once illuminated, not by an electric light overhead, but by dozens of electric candles.

I expected the room to smell musty, but instead there was a smell of something I couldn't quite identify, possibly mugwort with a hint of rosemary. The shelves were filled with books, mostly leather-bound volumes with gold embossing.

I turned to Edison. "This room is climate controlled!"

"It's necessary for these ancient volumes."

I nodded. "Of course." I walked around the room, marvelling at the ancient tomes. I stopped at a parchment sheet in a glass case.

"It's a page from the *Picatrix*," Edison told me. "An eleventh-century manuscript of astrology and magic."

"Do any of these volumes contain Old Magic?" I asked him.

Edison pointed to a set of volumes high on a

shelf.

"Do you think the murderer will break in and try to steal those?"

Edison appeared to be thinking it over for a moment. Finally, he spoke. "I'd be surprised if the murderer wanted those, because they're the history of Old Magic and the history of the Tuatha de Danann. The book that was stolen was a book of Old Magic spells."

I walked around the room, beside myself with excitement. There were so many beautiful old works in here. I read the names aloud, *Papyri Graecae Magicae*; *Liber Razielis Archangeli*; *The Sworn Book of Honorius; Clavicula Salomonis*.

"I'll teach you the incantations so you can have access to this room," Edison told me.

"Really?"

He nodded. "You are the one who should be the keeper of this room. You are the Bookmarker, after all. But for now, we should be getting back to the others. We don't want Harriet to suspect anything."

As I turned around to walk out, JenniFur ran between my legs, almost tripping me up. "I didn't see you in here," I exclaimed.

"That is because I didn't know if I was

allowed in here," she admitted.

"Yes, of course you're allowed in here."

JenniFur ran into the living room, and I followed her more slowly, with Edison behind me.

I needn't have worried. Harriet was staring fixedly at the TV, playing some sort of video game. Delilah was sitting on the floor beside her, clearly enthralled by what Harriet was doing, and Daphne was sitting on the sofa, reading a book and muttering to herself.

I was worried about Caspian. Where was he? Detective Stevens hadn't called. Caspian himself hadn't come to my apartment.

The knock on the door flooded me with relief. "Caspian!" I said aloud. I hurried to the door. Edison put a restraining hand on my shoulder, but I shook it off.

I flung open the door, but to my dismay, it was not Caspian who was standing there, but Prudence.

She was wringing her hands nervously, and her face was white and drawn.

"Nell, I have a message for you," she said. "It's from a new ghost."

All the blood ran from my head. "Caspian!" I squeaked.

CHAPTER 6

I grabbed Edison's shoulder for support. My knees buckled.

"He said his name was Emerson," Prudence said.

Relief washed over me in waves. "You haven't heard from Caspian?"

Prudence appeared puzzled. "Detective Cole?" I nodded. She pushed on. "No, why?"

"He went missing earlier today," I told her. "I'm minding his niece until he's found. Anyway, please come inside. Let's go into the kitchen. I don't want his niece to overhear anything," I added in hushed tones.

Daphne and Delilah looked up, but I signalled

to them to stay where they were. They both nodded, although Daphne did not look pleased at all.

Once in the kitchen, Prudence said, "I'm sorry, I should have brought you all some coffee. I was just so shocked when the ghost appeared."

I waved her concerns away. "I can make you some coffee if you'd like some, but it won't be anywhere near as good as yours."

Prudence nodded weakly. "Yes, that would be good, thanks." She clutched her stomach. "It was quite a shock."

I looked in the fridge and took out a plate of cupcakes Daphne and Delilah had given me the day before. I put them on the table. "You might need carbs and sugar after your shock."

"I never say no to carbs and sugar," Prudence said with a chuckle. I was relieved to see some colour was returning to her face.

While the coffee was brewing, I popped into the living room. "I'm making coffee. Would anyone like some, or maybe tea?"

"Coffee, please," Daphne and Delilah said, but Harriet did not respond. I took that as a no.

When everybody, apart from Harriet, had coffee, and everybody, including Harriet, had a cupcake, I took my seat at the table opposite Prudence.

"I didn't open the café today, but I was doing some paperwork when a ghost appeared to me."

I gasped. "You could see him?"

Prudence shook her head. "Oh no! I didn't mean I could see him with my natural eyes. Levi is the only ghost I have ever seen with my natural eyes."

I remembered Prudence had told me Levi was the first ghost she had ever seen with her own eyes, but it turned out he was not a ghost, but rather, he was in a coma, and his spirit had appeared to her. When Levi came out of the coma, they met and subsequently married. It was a wonderful love story. I was broken out of my reverie when I realised Prudence had asked me a question.

"I'm sorry, what was that?"

"I asked you if you knew Emerson?"

"Not as well as Edison did. Not at all, really. Did you know him, Prudence?"

"Yes, he came to the café for coffee all the time. He appeared to me—that is, to my spiritual senses—only five or so minutes ago."

Edison spoke up for the first time. "Did Emerson tell you who murdered him?"

Prudence shook her head. "No, he didn't see anybody."

I was trying to frame some questions, but I had to be careful. Prudence had no idea we were Seelie. "Go on," I said in encouraging tones.

"He appeared and told me he had been murdered."

"And he didn't see who did it?" Edison asked again.

Prudence sipped her coffee before responding. "No, I asked him that. He said he didn't see anybody. I asked him if he had any clue who did it, and he said he didn't."

Edison sighed. "That was my next question."

"And he didn't tell me how he was murdered," Prudence said.

Edison shot a look at me. "The doctor said he died of natural causes, so I can only assume it was a poison of some kind," Edison told her.

"But you didn't seem shocked when I told you he was murdered?" Prudence frowned.

"I had my suspicions," Edison told her. "The only thing is, I didn't think Emerson had any enemies, and I'm absolutely clueless as to who it could be. I've discussed it with Nell."

I smiled and shrugged.

"There's one more thing," Prudence said. "He said the murderer stole his book."

That seemed strange to me. "Did the murderer steal the book before or after he or she murdered Emerson?" I asked her.

At first, Prudence seemed surprised by my question, but then she nodded slowly. "Oh, I see what you mean. If the book was stolen *before* Emerson was murdered, then he would have seen the murderer, and if the book was stolen *after* he was murdered, his ghost should have seen the murderer."

I nodded. "Yes, that's what I meant."

"I assume the book was stolen after he was murdered," Prudence said. "When people are murdered, they often don't remember the events surrounding their murder or the events immediately afterwards. That's typical. He said he had borrowed the book from you, from your bookstore, Nell."

I was surprised the ghost had given her so much information. I looked at Edison.

To my relief, he took over the conversation. "Yes, Emerson liked to borrow some of the rarer books written in ancient languages. They wouldn't have been of any real value though and certainly wouldn't be worth a fortune. I'm sure that couldn't have been the motive for murder."

"The main thing Emerson wanted to tell you," Prudence continued, "was that he had the strong impression that the murderer didn't want any other books in your bookstore, Nell. He didn't want you to worry that you are in danger too."

"That was kind of him to think of me at such a time," I said.

Prudence stood up. "I had better get back to Levi. He doesn't like me having anything to do with murder investigations, you see. It's put my life in danger in the past."

"Thanks so much for your help. I really appreciate it." I stood up too.

"One more thing," Edison said. "I know Emerson didn't see the murderer, but if his ghost turns up again, could you ask him if he let anybody into his house this morning."

Prudence plated her palm on her forehead. "Oh, I forgot to tell you that. I asked him if there was anybody in his house at the time, and he said there wasn't."

"Then the murderer wasn't known to him," I suggested.

Edison rubbed his chin. "Possibly. Possibly," he said again.

CHAPTER 7

*I*t had been a long day. I had called Detective Sam Stevens, but he had not been at all forthcoming. He simply told me that he didn't know where Caspian was and that he would call me as soon as he had any information. My attempts to press him were futile.

Harriet had played games all day. She was reluctant to speak to anybody, no doubt upset by the disappearance of her uncle. To make matters worse, Edison remained convinced that Caspian's disappearance had nothing to do with Emerson's murder.

The day was dreary, cold and overcast with drizzling rain. It did nothing to improve my mood, which was one of melancholy.

It was with relief that I showered and dressed, ready to go to Daphne and Delilah's for dinner and to stay the night. When I emerged from my bedroom, Harriet was still playing a game. "We should leave now," I told her.

She stood up, carefully deposited her game consoles into her bag, and grabbed her backpack.

I took an umbrella from the umbrella stand by the front door and stepped into the rain. When I made to hold it over Harriet, she ducked away. "Only old people have umbrellas," she said with disdain.

"Old and *nicely dry* people," I muttered.

"Pick me up!" JenniFur said. "Cats don't like to get wet."

I shrugged and made my way to Daphne and Delilah's house, with Harriet trudging reluctantly behind me, and me struggling to hold JenniFur as well as the umbrella over the two of us.

When I reached the comfort of the dry porch, I put JenniFur down and raised my hand to knock. Before I had a chance to do so, the door flew open, and Delilah was standing there, resplendent in a skin-tight, bright orange jumpsuit. The tinfoil hat on her head was sporting two bright yellow antennas with a fluffy yellow pom-pom perched at the top of each one.

It was all I could do not to gasp. The whole impression was heightened by the overly strong, heady aroma of musk and floral perfume. I suspected she had used a whole bottle, maybe five.

"Come in!"

Harriet pushed past me. "Thanks."

As I stepped into the house, I heard Harriet gasp. "Wow!" That was followed by, "This is insane! The house is divided into two parts!"

I walked into the room to see Harriet smiling from ear to ear. It was the first time she had looked happy since I had met her. "I love it!" she exclaimed. "This side must be yours, Ms Dimples?"

"You can call me Delilah."

Daphne stepped into the room. "But you can call *me* Ms Dimples. Yes, that unseemly side of the room belongs to Delilah, while my side of the room is tasteful and refined."

Both JenniFur and Harriet ignored her. JenniFur ran to a fluffy cushion and stretched out on it, while Harriet ran over to the space age chair hanging from the ceiling. She wasted no time sitting on it. "This is cool." Soon, the chair was swinging wildly.

I handed Daphne the bottle of wine I had brought.

"Thank you," she said, "but I suspect we'll all need something stronger."

For once, I agreed with her.

Daphne ushered me into the dining room where Edison was sitting.

"Where's Harriet?" he asked me.

"She's testing the structural fortitude of my roof by swinging from that crazy chair of Delilah's," Daphne said tersely.

Edison chuckled. "As soon as dinner is over, Delilah could maybe show Harriet to her room, and she could play games while we discuss the case."

His suggestion was met with a murmur of agreement.

"I must say, I'm relieved that Emerson's ghost said the murderer was only after that book and isn't interested in any other of our volumes," I said.

Edison nodded. "We don't have any other Old Magic spell books, but the murderer wouldn't know that. Still, it does seem as though the murderer was only after that one book, which of course is such an incredibly rare find, being filled with Old Magic spells."

"But it's of no use to anybody who can't read languages that are millennia old," I protested.

"Precisely. If you'll excuse me, I'll fetch dinner." With that, Daphne left the room.

I looked up at Delilah. "Why don't you sit?" She was standing there, hovering over me.

"I can't possibly sit down," she said. "This jumpsuit is far too tight. I had to put on my strongest shapewear to get it on, and it hasn't really helped."

"Why don't you change into something else for dinner?" I suggested.

Delilah appeared doubtful. "But fashion isn't meant to feel good, it's only meant to *look* good."

"But it will be hard for you to eat dinner standing up," I pointed out. "And it will be easier for you to give us your valuable input into the case if you're sitting down."

The flattery seemed to work. "I take your point. I'll be right back."

Daphne reappeared, clutching a large plate. "Where is Delilah? I wanted her to help me bring out the food."

"She's changing into something that will enable her to sit down," I said.

Daphne rolled her eyes, deposited the plate on the table, and walked back into the kitchen, muttering to herself. I couldn't hear what she was saying, but I figured that was for the best.

Delilah appeared moments later, this time wearing a flowing gown covered with peacock feathers. When she saw me staring, she said, "This is made from discarded peacock feathers, not feathers plucked from the poor peacocks themselves." She went into a lengthy explanation of how, when, and why peacocks drop their feathers, but I wasn't listening. I was consumed with worry for Caspian. Where was he? Why wasn't anybody doing anything about it? Or did Detective Stevens know what was going on and simply wasn't telling me?

"And that's why peacocks make that strange sound," Delilah concluded. "Did you hear everything I said, Nell?"

"Yes," I lied. "Daphne was looking for you."

Delilah hurried into the kitchen, her peacock feathers rustling behind her.

Soon, the table was laden with crispy, aromatic garlic bread, a huge platter of lasagne, and every type of salad imaginable. Daphne filled the adults' glasses with wine and another glass with lemonade for Harriet, who was presently summoned to the table.

"I hope you like lasagne," Daphne said to her.

It seems she did, as she wasted no time piling it onto her plate. I noted she didn't touch the salad, although she appeared fond of the garlic bread. I thought she would complain that she had to drink lemonade and not wine, but it seemed I had misjudged her.

Harriet finished her meal when I was only about one-third of the way through mine. "Can I go to my room now?" she asked Delilah. "The one with the big TV?"

"But there's ice cream," Delilah protested.

Harriet's face fell, but Delilah soon added, "Come on, I'll show you to your room, and you can set up your games. I'll bring in your ice cream when it's ready."

Harriet beamed from ear to ear and followed Delilah out of the room.

"Thank goodness we're rid of the kid," Daphne said. "Now we can discuss the murder case over dinner like civilised people."

"Shouldn't we wait for Delilah to get back?" I asked her.

"I suppose so."

As soon as Delilah returned, the conversation at once turned to Emerson's murder.

"Since our cakery was shut for the day, Delilah and I have discussed it at length, and we have come up with three suspects," Daphne said. "First and foremost, Nora Beckett, the horrible cleaning lady. A most abominable woman. She's so rude. When she buys cakes from the shop, she simply grunts at us. She has the most appalling manners—or rather, no manners at all."

"But that doesn't mean she's a murderer," Edison pointed out.

Daphne ignored him and kept speaking. "And then there is Dr Logan Tate. He and Emerson were close. They went to the pub every Friday night."

Edison shook his head. "That is, unless Emerson was going to a football game that fell on a Friday night."

Daphne nodded. "Precisely. And that leads me to my last suspect, Algerone Riverty. Emerson and Algerone went to football games together on a regular basis. Now, Edison, do you have any suspects to add to that list?"

Edison shook his head. He pulled a notebook from his pocket and placed it on the table. "Those are the very three suspects I myself came up with today. Nora Beckett had access to Emerson's household. Logan and Algerone were also regular visitors to Emerson's house."

I was appalled. "But these three people were good friends of his, weren't they? Could he have been murdered by a close friend?"

"Nora Beckett wasn't his close friend," Daphne said. "She was his cleaning lady. I suspect her."

"You've already said that a thousand times," Delilah said. "It's getting old, Daphne. You only suspect her because you don't like her."

"Disliked people can be murderers too," Daphne snapped. "Just because I dislike her, doesn't mean she's not a murderer."

My head was spinning.

"What does JenniFur think?" Edison asked me.

JenniFur looked up from her bowl of salmon. "The butler did it."

They all looked at me. "What did she say?" Edison asked me.

I sighed. "She said the butler did it."

To JenniFur, I said, "There *is* no butler."

"She means the cleaning lady, obviously!" Daphne raised her eyebrows.

I knew JenniFur was simply making a throwaway remark, but to settle the issue, I asked her, "Do you think the cleaning lady did it?"

"What cleaning lady? Please don't disturb me when I'm eating salmon."

"She knows nothing about a cleaning lady," I told them. "She's concentrating on eating her salmon."

Daphne's eyes narrowed. She looked most displeased.

"JenniFur, when you've finished your salmon, would you mind going to Harriet's room to keep an eye on her?" I asked her. "And run out and tell me if she leaves her room. We don't want her listening in to our conversation again."

JenniFur was licking her paw, but immediately stopped and trotted off in the direction of Harriet's room.

"What if it was somebody else entirely?" I asked.

Edison stroked his long, white beard. "I've given that a lot of thought. For a start, I think it had to be somebody who knew Emerson's habits, namely, that he would borrow books from the bookstore."

Daphne chimed in. "That's right, but I don't think the murderer knew that the bookshop had an Old Magic grimoire in its possession."

Edison hurried to agree with her. "That's right. Otherwise, the bookstore would have been the target. No, I've thought this through until my head spins. I suspect the murderer saw the Old Magic spell book and decided to do away with Emerson on the spot."

"But didn't the murderer need time to prepare?" I asked him. "I mean, given the murderer killed Emerson with Old Magic, it would take time to prepare."

"Emerson borrowed that book about five days before he was murdered," Edison told me.

I nodded. "I see. So, the murderer could have seen the book at any time over those five days and cooked up a plan to murder him and steal the book."

The others all nodded vigorously.

"That's why it has to be the cleaning lady, that

nasty, dreadful woman." Daphne narrowed her eyes. "She cleaned his house on a regular basis, and she would have seen the book."

"Not necessarily," Edison said. "I'm sure Emerson didn't leave it lying around, out in the open."

"Were any of his friends Seelie too?" I asked. "If they were, maybe he mentioned it to them."

Daphne took a large gulp of wine before speaking. "As far as I know, that dreadful woman, Logan Tate, and Algerone Riverty are not Seelie."

Now I was thoroughly confused. "But can only Seelies use Old Magic?"

"You're confusing Nell," Delilah said. To me, she added, "What Daphne was trying to say was that we don't know if any are Seelie, but obviously one of them is and is the murderer. This person has kept the fact that they're Seelie hidden."

"Which means they're of the Night Court but are hiding it from everybody," Daphne added.

I wondered how long it would take her to blame the Night Court. Daphne, Delilah, and Edison were of the Summer Court, and there was no love lost between the Summer Court and the Night Court. I still didn't know why.

"I'm certain this has something to do with

Caspian's disappearance," I said. I held up my hands, palms to the ceiling. "Why isn't anybody else worried about this? He wouldn't leave his niece alone in the house. Something has clearly happened to him!"

Delilah reached across and patted my hand. "I'm sure his partner, that nice Detective What's-his-face is looking for him."

"Stevens," I supplied.

"No dear, my name is Delilah. Clearly, you're overcome with worry."

I wiped my hand over my brow and then drained the rest of my wine in one go. "No, Caspian's partner is Detective Stevens."

"That's nice," Delilah said absently.

Daphne rolled her eyes. "All right then. Nell, on the off chance that your detective's disappearance is linked in any way to Emerson's murder, then finding his murderer will lead you to the detective."

For the first time since Caspian had disappeared, my spirits lifted.

Daphne pushed on. "We need to ask Emerson's neighbours if they saw anything, although we will have to be discreet, because everybody thinks his death was natural causes.

Unless we can think of somebody else, we have to focus on the suspects. We'll need to investigate Nora Beckett, Logan Tate, and Algerone Riverty."

We all agreed that it was a good idea.

Daphne stood. "I'll clear the table and fetch the ice cream. I've also made some lemon meringue pie." She held up her right hand in front of her. "I don't want any help. You three spend your time discussing the case."

Just then, JenniFur ran in and jumped on my lap. Her hair was standing on end.

"It's an emergency!" she squealed.

CHAPTER 8

"**W**hat is it?" I jumped to my feet.

"Harriet's on her way to listen in."

I breathed a huge sigh of relief. "JenniFur! I thought something terrible had happened."

"It would have been terrible if she overheard all your spy talk and Seelie talk and murder talk, obviously," JenniFur said with disdain. "I thought you would be grateful."

"I *am* grateful. Thank you." To the others, I said, "Harriet is on her way to listen in."

"I'll thwart her with ice cream and lemon meringue pie." Daphne hurried to the kitchen.

Edison, Delilah, and I made small talk. We tried to make it as boring as possible. We spoke at length about the weather, about how we always had too much rain or not enough. It was enough to bore anybody, and hopefully it was boring Harriet right now.

Daphne returned with a bowl filled with lemon meringue pie and ice cream. "Would you take this to Harriet, Delilah?" She shoved the bowl at her sister.

I heard footsteps hurrying in the other direction and bit back a smile. "JenniFur, would you check on Harriet again?"

"I will, if you will be grateful."

"Thank you. I'll be ever so grateful."

With that, JenniFur stalked off in the direction of Harriet's room.

"Then the first person we need to investigate should be Nora Beckett, since she obviously did it," Daphne said. "But we will have to be careful questioning her, in case she's still on a murderous rampage."

"I think Nell should be the one to interrogate her," Edison said.

My hand flew to my throat. "Why me?" I squealed.

"I believe my reasons are quite sound," Edison said. "If she is a Seelie and the murderer, then she would know that Daphne, Delilah, and I are Seelie. She will be suspicious of our questioning. However, you haven't been in town for long, and I doubt she would know you are Seelie."

I made to protest, but Edison pushed on. "You can go there and tell her that your book is missing. Tell her that the police say Emerson's death was of natural causes, but you can't understand what happened to the book. Say that it's a valuable book and that I had lent to him, unbeknownst to you. Tell her that you want to get it back."

"That's a good idea," Daphne said. "You can pretend you're simply interested in the whereabouts of the book."

"But Nell *is* interested in the whereabouts of the book, of course." Delilah glared at her sister.

"That's not what I meant, and you know it, Delilah," Daphne snapped. "Of course, Nell wants to know where the book is, but she also wants to know who the murderer is. The Where will tell us Who, as we already know the Why."

"Do you think she kidnapped Caspian?" Before anyone could answer, I continued hurriedly. "But why? Why would she kidnap him? There have been no ransom demands—not as far as I know, anyway—and Detective Stevens said Caspian wasn't working on any particular case at the moment."

"Maybe Detective Stevens was lying to you," Edison suggested.

I nodded. "Yes, I had considered that possibility, but if Caspian is connected with Emerson's murder, then the murderer has kidnapped him. I can't figure out why."

"Possibly because Nora Beckett is completely unhinged," Daphne said. "Maybe she kidnapped him and locked him in a dark room for a few months until this all blows over."

"But why?" Delilah asked.

"Isn't it obvious, Delilah?"

"If it was obvious, I wouldn't have asked you," Delilah retorted.

Daphne snorted. "Because he's a *homicide* detective. She kidnapped him a short time after she murdered Emerson so he wouldn't be able to investigate the case."

"But the doctor said Emerson died of natural causes," Edison pointed out.

Daphne tapped her chin. "Well, maybe she was afraid he would change his mind."

I ate a huge mouthful of lemon meringue pie.

Junk food made everything seem better. I didn't know if lemon meringue pie could be technically considered to be junk food, but it was certainly a dessert absolutely filled with fat and sugar. That had to be a plus.

"And there's another reason I think Nora Beckett is the murderer." Daphne paused, no doubt for dramatic effect, and looked at each one of us in turn.

Finally, I could stand it no longer. "Why?" I asked her.

Daphne allowed herself a small smile of satisfaction. "Because she's a house cleaner. She would have access to many houses on Wild Lime Mountain, and she could snoop. If she was an undercover agent, she could bide her time for years cleaning peoples' houses and snooping, waiting for something to turn up that she could use to her own advantage. After all, Wild Lime Mountain has a higher Seelie population than any other town in Australia."

Most of what she said made sense to me, but one thing didn't. I voiced my concerns. "What do you mean by undercover agent?"

"The Anvil and Reed," Edison said. "Remember, Nell, I told you about an ancient organisation that was supposed to be in the myths of time, but rumours have said it has currently restarted?"

"Yes, but I'd almost forgotten it."

"It's my belief that the murderer is part of this sect."

"What do they want?" I asked him.

He shrugged. "Who would know? But they certainly want to cause chaos and disruption. The Anvil and Reed used Old Magic centuries ago."

"Yes, it has to be them," Daphne said.

"This is a lot for me to take in," I admitted. "Now, this book of Old Magic, how long would it take somebody to translate the spells in it?"

The three of them chuckled. "Possibly never," Edison said. "That is the language of the Tuatha de Danann. Nobody has spoken that language for millennia."

"But if it is impossible to translate, why did the murderer steal the book?"

"Because it seems that it is *not* impossible to translate." Daphne's tone was solemn. "Maybe the murderer thought there was a chance of translating it."

"I'm afraid that must be the case," Edison said. "I have no idea how, but nobody would murder a man to steal a book that was worthless to them. It only stands to reason that the murderer thought there was a way to translate the spells."

"That can't be good," I muttered. "Not good at all."

Edison gasped and jumped to his feet. "It happened just then! A burst of it!"

We all stared at him.

Daphne's long, bony fingers closed around his arm. "What happened?"

"Old Magic!"

CHAPTER 9

*E*dison stood, frozen to the spot. It was as though he had been turned into a statue. I thought he was having some sort of medical episode and rushed over to him, but Daphne placed a restraining hand on my arm.

"He's okay—he sensed a power surge, apparently," she told me.

Edison shook himself. His face had paled. "Old Magic," he said.

"Has somebody else been murdered?" I asked. It was the first thing that came to mind.

Edison was trembling. Daphne and Delilah helped him to a comfortable chair on Daphne's side of the living room.

"I don't know," Edison said, "but it was

nowhere near as strong as the Old Magic I felt this morning, when Emerson was murdered."

"Should we drive to each of the suspects' houses so you can see if you can pick up some vestiges of the Old Magic?" I asked him.

"That's a good idea," Delilah said, but Daphne shook her head.

"No, that could be exactly what the murderer wants."

"What do you mean?" Edison asked her.

"Maybe the murderer wants to know if there is a Hierophant amongst us. A Hierophant would be the major adversary to somebody practising Old Magic."

Edison nodded slowly. "I see. You think that surge was to draw me out, rather, to draw out any Hierophant in town."

"Precisely." Daphne patted Edison on his shoulder.

"But Edison, you went to Emerson's house this morning when you felt the power surge," I said. "If the murderer wanted to get rid of a Hierophant, wouldn't they have stayed around to see who turned up, watching from a distance?"

"Possibly, but I was a regular visitor to Emerson's house."

I persisted with my theory. "Even so, if nobody else turned up that would have to point to you being a Hierophant."

Edison disagreed with me. "No, not at all. Hierophants are most uncommon. The murderer would have no idea there is a Hierophant on Wild Lime Mountain."

I was beginning to catch on. "I see. So, if the murderer *did* suspect that you might be a Hierophant, given that you went to Emerson's shortly after he was murdered by Old Magic, the murderer might have produced that burst of Old Magic now to see if you would go around town looking for the source?"

Edison, Daphne, and Delilah all nodded.

"That seems to be the logical explanation," Edison said, "given that the only other Old Magic I have ever detected ever in my entire life, was when Emerson was murdered."

"Then I had better be very careful questioning Nora Beckett. I don't want her to use Old Magic on me." I noticed my hands were shaking, so I sat on them.

"We couldn't let you go if we thought you'd be in any danger," Daphne said. "Your book is missing, so it's quite natural that you would ask her if she knew anything about it."

"I suppose so."

I spent a sleepless night at Daphne and Delilah's. My bed was comfortable, possibly because I was in Daphne's spare room furnished with a lovely soft bed and soft furnishings in pretty chintz patterns.

Still, I was dreadfully worried about Caspian. Detective Stevens would call me as soon as Caspian was found, and as I hadn't heard from him, it was clear Caspian was still missing. What if something terrible had happened to him, something worse than being kidnapped?

I tossed and turned. In the little sleep I did have, I had disturbing dreams. I dreamt I was in a post-apocalyptic town looking for my car in the car park. The car park extended into a terrifying dystopian town, and night was falling. I awoke, tossed and turned some more, and then had the same dream.

After breakfast, I went to speak with Nora Beckett, while Harriet and JenniFur stayed with Daphne and Delilah. Edison had described the missing book to me at great length.

I had been nervous the night before, but I

wasn't nervous now. If she was the murderer, then she could lead me to Caspian. That spurred me on.

I only hoped she would be home and not out on a job.

Nora Beckett's house was on the edge of town, near the main road but tucked away in a little street that afforded each house plenty of privacy. When I got out of the car, I looked towards the coast. I had been able to see spectacular views of Surfers Paradise on the way there, but the thick bushland between here and the coast in this spot made views from Nora Beckett's street impossible.

I walked to her front door, steeling myself.

I had only knocked once when Nora Beckett opened the door. She looked me up and down and then grunted, "I'm fully booked. You'll have to find somebody else."

"I don't want my house cleaned," I said.

She was in the process of shutting the door in my face, but she paused and stared at me.

"I'm Nell Darling, the owner of the *It's A Likely Story* bookshop," I told her. "Could I speak with you? I won't take up much of your time."

Nora grunted again and opened the door. The

door opened onto a small, dark room, a closed-in front porch. The next room was the living room. It too was small, tiny in fact, but it was as neat as a pin. I had expected that most house cleaners would have untidy houses–I had heard many jokes to that effect, such as plumbers needing plumbing work done in their own houses and the like—but it certainly wasn't the situation in Nora's case. Everything was highly polished, and there wasn't one speck of dust to be found.

Nora indicated I should sit on a brown sofa covered with a throw rug made from multicoloured crochet squares. "Would you like a cup of tea? I was just about to have one."

I was about to accept, but then I thought she might poison me. Instead, I said, "No, thank you. I've just had one. Please, you go ahead." Still, I felt a little dizzy for some reason and could have done with the sugar.

Nora grunted and shuffled out of the room, I presume to the kitchen. I took the opportunity to study the room. There was nothing that gave the slightest indication of magic. Everything appeared entirely mundane. Opposite me was a wood combustion fireplace with a gleaming copper flue. The walls were a faded pink-beige colour, and the two armchairs were brown and also covered in crochet squares. There was no floor rug, just wooden floorboards which were not polished. There was a sour smell in the air which I couldn't quite identify. There was also the unmistakable and unpleasant odour of mould.

Nora seemed an assuming person, the last person I would consider to be a murderer. Her lifestyle seemed simple, one of honest hard work. If she was a murderer and involved with Old Magic, then she was hiding it well. Nothing in her living room gave the slightest indication that she was a Seelie or into magic of any kind, and given that I had arrived without warning, she wouldn't have had time to conceal anything.

Nora returned to the living room, clutching a ceramic mug of tea. She sat opposite me in an armchair and placed her cup of tea on a coaster on top of a yellowing lace doily.

She looked at me expectantly and then asked, "What did you want to speak to me about?"

All at once, a pang of nervousness hit me. I rubbed my forehead. Did I have migraine coming on? I swallowed loudly and said, "I suppose you know that Emerson Mortcombe died yesterday?"

She nodded. I pushed on. "He had borrowed

a valuable, rare book from my bookshop. I didn't even know he had borrowed it. My manager, Edison, only told me yesterday. I didn't even know anybody borrowed books from my shop. I mean, Prudence, the lady who owns the café next door, borrows books in exchange for coffee, but I had no idea anyone else borrowed books."

I realised I was rambling, so I took a deep breath and let it out slowly before continuing. "Edison went to Emerson's house to fetch the book back and found Emerson had passed away, but he didn't see the book."

"Well, I didn't steal it," Nora snapped. A malevolent look passed across her face. "I don't steal things." She looked at me with glittery eyes, which had formed into slits. "Only last week, that new rich woman who has moved to town got me to clean her house. I found twenty dollars in a drawer. I knew she had put it there just to test me to see if I would steal it. The nerve of her!"

I hurried to reassure her. "Oh no, nobody stole it, least of all you. Nobody thinks that," I lied. "No, Emerson obviously put it somewhere for safekeeping. I was hoping you could tell me if you had seen it in an unusual place."

She didn't say anything, so I asked, "Did you see the book anywhere?"

She was still regarding me with suspicion. "What did it look like? Emerson has, I mean had, plenty of books. He loved books. He had all sorts of strange books on his bookshelves. I'm sure they wouldn't have been interesting reading, but Emerson seemed to think that they were."

"This was a large book," I told her. I showed her the size with my hands. "And it was about so thick." I held my index finger and thumb apart. "It was a leather-bound book with gold writing on the cover. Emerson would have worn gloves when he read it."

She nodded. "Emerson often read books with gloves. That stopped them from being damaged, the old books I mean."

I nodded, relieved that she seemed to have calmed down. "Did you see such a book?"

"I was at his house the day before yesterday, in the morning," she said. "He told me not to clean in his study because he was working on something difficult and didn't want to be disturbed. Maybe it was that book. Still, that Dr Tate visited him that day, and he didn't tell him to go away. He let *him* into his study. The nerve!"

"Did you happen to see the book?" I asked her.

She shook her head. "No! He asked me not to disturb him, so I didn't! I'm not in the habit of disturbing people." She shot me a particularly nasty glare.

"No, of course not," I said, shooting her a wide smile. It was not returned.

"Has somebody told you I disturb people?"

"Not at all," I said. "I was only asking because we don't know where the book is, and it's a valuable book. It really should be in a museum."

"Why is that?"

"Because it's old and rare," I said. "It's written in some ancient language that nobody can read."

She seemed to have lost interest in what I was saying and slurped her tea rather noisily. I waited for her to finish before asking, "Did he keep his rare books hidden? Maybe in a safe or something?"

"If he did, he didn't tell me," she said. "Why don't you go to his house and have a good look around?"

"I wouldn't like to do that," I told her. "I'll have to wait until the person who inherits everything comes to town."

"But Emerson told me he didn't have any living relatives," she said. "Who could possibly inherit?"

I shrugged. "I don't know. Surely, he left a will. Maybe he left his house and the contents to his friends."

"Academics!" she spat. "They never have any common sense. They can't make it in the real world, my mother always said. He didn't have any money, nothing to leave, only that old house of his and all those old books of his. All he was interested in were people who lived a long time ago, and who cares about them?"

I didn't know what to say, so I simply nodded. I tried to think of more questions I could ask, but my mind went blank.

The real murderer would surely try to find out if I was interested in the book because it was magic, that is, if I was Seelie or knew what the book really was, but Nora didn't ask me any questions at all. Not about the book at any rate. She seemed entirely defensive.

"Do you know Detective Cole?"

"Why? Do you think I'm a criminal?"

I shook my head. Nora was a most unpleasant

woman. "No, but he's a local, and he's gone missing."

"A friend of yours, is he?"

I was about to say he was but thought the better of it. "No, but I wanted to tell him about the missing book. As he's a local, I thought he might do something about it."

"He's gone missing, you say?"

"Yes."

"If he's a cop, why aren't the cops looking for him?"

I shrugged. "Maybe they are." I didn't want to give too much away.

A heavy silence fell upon us. I thought I should take my leave.

"Emerson's dead. It's a sad thing, isn't it?" Nora said after an interval.

"Yes, very sad. I didn't know Emerson."

Her eyebrows shot skyward. "You didn't know him? Why did you lend him the book?"

I had already explained that, but I hurried to explain it again. "I didn't lend him the book, Edison did."

She nodded vigorously. "Oh yes, you told me that."

"I didn't really know him," I added for good

measure.

"You already told me that." This time, her tone was accusatory.

I stood up. "Well, thank you for your time. I'm sorry about Emerson."

"Why are you sorry?"

"Well, because he's dead."

"But you said you didn't know him!"

"No, but I'm sorry when anybody dies."

She simply glared at me.

I smiled at her. I stood up and headed for her front door. I didn't see the metal chair in the way and tripped into it heavily, inadvertently pushing it along the floor for a distance. The noise it made as it scraped across her polished floor was ghastly, like fingernails on a blackboard.

"I'm so dreadfully sorry," I began, but when I looked down, there was not so much as a scratch on the floor. I stared in disbelief. The metal chair should have left deep scratches on the floor. I hurried to the door before she could berate me.

Nora opened the front door and slammed it behind me. I walked to my car. When I looked back, I could see her looking through the curtains at me. She quickly pulled them closed.

I drove away, and once I was out of sight, I

pressed the bluetooth on my car dashboard to call Edison.

"I was about to call you," he said by way of greeting. "Hurry back! Detective Stevens is here, and he wants to speak with you!"

CHAPTER 10

As soon as Edison spoke the words, the phone went dead. I tried to call him back, but nothing happened. I assumed there was no mobile phone service in this area.

Once I was back on the road from the coast to Wild Lime Mountain, I tried to call again. This time, there was a dial tone, but Edison didn't pick up.

It was only five or so minutes to the bookstore, but it seemed to take forever. I parked in my allocated parking spot and charged to the bookshop. Edison at once opened the door. "Detective Stevens is here, but Harriet is with Daphne and Delilah," he told me.

"What's it about?" I asked.

He shrugged. "He wouldn't tell me. I'll be in the kitchen if you need me."

I hurried to where Detective Stevens was, in the reading room. He was standing in front of the fireplace, although the fire had gone out.

"Have you found him?" I asked.

He shook his head. "No. I've come here to tell you that he's now officially missing. I thought I should tell you in person."

Despite the fact that Detective Stevens clearly thought he was doing me a favour by telling me the obvious in person, I was furious. "I *know* he's missing!" I said, doing my best not to yell. "I was the one who told you he was missing! Have you got any clues as to where he could be? Has there been a ransom note? What if somebody tries to kill him?"

I clutched at my stomach.

Detective Stevens appeared surprised at my outburst. "It's good that he's officially missing," he said in soothing tones, "because it gives us more ability to look for him."

I processed his words. "Do you have any clues as to where to start?"

"No. There were no fingerprints at the scene.

We asked the neighbours, but nobody saw anything."

"While his street isn't exactly a busy one, it still has a lot of houses on it," I said. "Surely, somebody saw something. He's a big strong man and a detective at that, so how did somebody kidnap him?"

Detective Stevens shrugged. "Maybe they said it was an emergency, and he had to go with them."

"But he wouldn't have left his phone behind or smashed a bottle of wine either," I pointed out. I knew the detective realised that—clearly, he was trying to placate me. "If you find out anything, anything at all, no matter how bad, would you please tell me?" I continued. "I'm still minding his niece, Harriet."

"Have you been in touch with her parents?"

I nodded. "Yes, Harriet called her father, and I spoke with him. He doesn't have a clue where Caspian is either."

"I see."

"Shouldn't you have been in touch with Caspian's half-brother, to find out if he knew something?"

"Yes, that's one of the reasons I came here, to

get his number from you. I could have called to ask for it, but I want to tell you in person that the case has been upgraded to a missing person case."

"Thank you. I'll text his number to you now. Hang on a moment." I tapped the contacts on my phone and shared the number to Detective Stevens's phone.

"What do you know about the relationship between Detective Cole and his half-brother?"

"He said he only found out about him a few years ago. Wait, you don't think his brother has anything to do with his disappearance?"

"We have to pursue all avenues."

"I see. But if he was going to kidnap or do something to Caspian, why would he do it when his own daughter was here? He must know that would upset her."

"Like I said, we have to pursue all avenues." With that, he nodded to me and walked towards the door. I hurried to open it for him and then shut it behind him.

Edison appeared. I filled him in on what had happened.

"Surely, he doesn't think his brother had anything to do with that," Edison said.

I shrugged. "Will you, Daphne, and Delilah

take it seriously now that Caspian is officially a missing person?"

Edison frowned and ran his hand over his brow. "Yes, Nell. I'm sorry I didn't take it more seriously at first, but I was distracted by Emerson's murder and the Old Magic."

"I still think the kidnapping and the murder could be linked."

Edison frowned deeply. "But how could that possibly be the case?"

"Maybe Caspian knew something about the identity of the murderer. He is a Seelie of the Night Court, after all."

Edison tapped his chin. "The timing *does* fit. Detective Cole went missing not long after Emerson was murdered. I just can't see how the two are related."

"That doesn't mean they're not related," I pointed out. "Hindsight is a wonderful thing. We'll probably only know after we solve the case and find Caspian."

"What happened with Nora Beckett?"

I planted my palm on my forehead. "Silly me! I was so distracted by Detective Stevens that I forgot all about her. She told me Emerson was working on a book in his study the day before he died, and he told her she wasn't to clean in his office that day."

"Did she say anything else?"

I shook my head. "She seemed awfully defensive about everything."

"What do you mean?"

"For example, she thought I was accusing her of stealing the book, stuff like that. She didn't say anything else about Emerson. Dr Tate was there that day, though."

"Was there anything in her house to indicate she might be Seelie?"

"Not at all. There was not a thing out of place. Not even a crystal or a set of tarot cards, not even a stick of incense. You couldn't have found a more mundane place if you tried."

"Do you think we can rule her out?"

I shrugged. "I don't like to rule anybody out, but I'd be surprised if she did it. I arrived at her place without warning, and she didn't have had time to hide anything. She's a most unpleasant person, though. I can see why Daphne has a problem with her."

"Would you like some more coffee?"

My mood improved considerably. "Did Prudence make some?"

Edison chuckled. "Her husband, Levi, has whisked her away to the Sunshine Coast for a few days. Apparently, he was most disconcerted that Emerson's ghost had connected with her."

I laughed, too. "If I were her, I'd be pretending I saw all manner of ghosts so I could go on lots of lovely holidays too."

"Well, my coffee isn't as good as Prudence's, but I've just made some," Edison said.

I followed him into the kitchen and sat down. "I'm so concerned that Caspian is still missing. Every TV show about kidnapping victims says that the first few hours are crucial, but nothing was done."

"If you're right and this is tied to Emerson's murder, then solving his murder will provide clues as to where Detective Cole is," Edison said. He scratched his head. "Though I can't possibly see the connection. Still, that doesn't mean we won't see it with time."

I slurped the coffee noisily, enjoying the feeling of my caffeine levels rising. "What do we do next?"

"Next on our list is Dr Logan Tate."

I sipped some more coffee before responding. "When you discovered Emerson's body and called

Dr Tate, you would have kept a close eye on him, surely? I mean, you must have been suspicious of everybody at that point."

"I was indeed," Edison said. "He didn't seem to do anything untoward."

"Why did you call him specifically? There are several doctors in town."

"Because Emerson had a landline phone on his desk, a funny old green one, and the doctor's name was written on a sticky note attached to the phone."

"And did you find Emerson's body at his desk?"

Edison nodded.

"But don't you think that's suspicious? What if he murdered Emerson and then put his number on the sticky note next to Emerson's body to make sure you'd call him."

Edison appeared to be thinking it over. "But I don't think it would have made a difference, really. Any doctor in town would have said it was natural causes. None of them are Seelie, to my knowledge."

I finished the coffee and poured myself another one. I sat back down at the table before voicing my concerns. "But what if he wanted to know if who the Hierophant was? I mean, what if he wanted to find out if there was a Hierophant in town? He knew any Hierophant would sense that Old Magic was used to kill Emerson, so he put his phone number next to Emerson's body, knowing that whoever called him was likely the Hierophant."

Edison scooped a spoon of sugar into his coffee, even though he had already drunk half of it, and stirred it in well. "Oh dear. I see what you mean. Still, I did tell him I was there to pick up a book from Emerson."

"That was clever, to cover your tracks."

"I wasn't thinking of covering my tracks at the time," Edison admitted. "I was worried about the book being missing, and I thought the doctor would have seen it."

"But obviously he hadn't seen it," I said.

There was a knock on the shop door even though the sign was flipped to Closed. Edison and I hurried to the door. There, standing on the step, was none other than Doctor Logan Tate.

"Dr Tate!" Edison said with obvious surprise. "Did you want to buy a book?"

The doctor chuckled. "No, I was coming to see you about the funeral arrangements."

"I'm Nell Darling, the owner of the bookstore," I told him.

Edison's hand flew to his mouth. "Oh, how rude of me. Sorry, I didn't realise you two haven't met."

The doctor and I smiled at each other. Edison pushed on. "Who is organising the funeral? Emerson said he didn't have any relatives."

"His lawyer contacted me as I was the attending physician. He said there were no provisions in Emerson's will for a funeral."

"But what does that mean?" I asked him. "Emerson has to have a funeral."

The doctor turned his attention to me. "Was he a particular friend of yours?"

I shook my head. "No, I'd never met him, but that doesn't mean he shouldn't have a funeral."

The doctor chuckled. "Quite so, quite so. The community will rally and provide a funeral for him. He will be buried in the local cemetery."

"But surely there will be a service?" I persisted.

The doctor nodded. "Most certainly. Edison, will you help?"

"Of course, I'll help," Edison said. "But there's something I wanted to ask you, Dr Tate. I had lent Emerson a very valuable book owned by the bookstore, and it is missing."

The doctor looked shocked. "Missing you say? Valuable?"

"Yes, it's a rare book. I went there to fetch the book but found poor Emerson dead, and there was no sign of the book. Nell, of course, is quite concerned."

"It was kind of you to lend him such a rare book in the first place," Dr Tate said to me.

Edison and I exchanged glances. "I'm afraid Nell didn't know anything about it. I was the one who lent him the book," Edison said. "He borrowed many books over the years. You know what he was like with ancient languages."

The doctor nodded slowly. "I do indeed. It was a passion of his. Well, if you'll excuse me, I'll be on my way. I'll be in touch about the funeral. We're going to take up a collection. It will be on the Wild Lime Mountain community page on Facebook."

Edison and I looked at each other. "Do you suspect him?" I asked him after Dr Tate had left. "I'm sure we will have to investigate him further."

"We certainly will," Edison said. "Nell, I'm a little uneasy about the other books in the secret room. Despite what Emerson's ghost said, I'm worried someone might have broken in last night to steal them, when nobody was here. It's not logical, as the history of Old Magic will be of no use to anybody, but I want to check if they're still there, to put my mind at rest."

Edison and walked to the secret room. He did the incantation, and the door materialised. With another incantation, the door opened.

"Don't forget you're going to teach me those incantations," I told him.

"Of course, of course," Edison muttered absently. He climbed the ladder to fetch a book from a top shelf.

When he was at the bottom of the ladder, he handed the book to me. I took it and placed it on the table in front of me. "What is it?" I asked him.

"This is a book of the history of Old Magic," Edison said, jabbing his gloved finger on the title.

"You can read that?" I was incredulous. The script looked like a cross between Coptic and cuneiform.

Edison chuckled. "No, no, of course not. We were able to make guess based on the illustrations."

"Is it safe to open the book?"

Edison waved one hand at me. "Of course." He handed me a pair of white gloves.

I put them on and opened the book. It was beautiful, with gold leaf edges along with illuminated illustrations of brilliant colours and intricate designs. Some pictures were in miniature.

"The gold here is both leaf and powdered form," Edison told me. "Plus, this one also has silver, and silver was rarer than gold in illuminated manuscripts."

"How old is it?"

"This book is likely a seventeenth-century copy of a far earlier work. In fact, there were probably numerous copies over the centuries," Edison told me. "Illuminated manuscripts were produced between the twelfth and seventeenth centuries. It was monasteries that first produced them."

"It's beautiful." I was about to say more, when I noticed Edison's face had turned white, and he was staring past me.

I spun around.

Harriet was standing in the doorway. I gasped.

Before I could do or say anything, she put JenniFur down and walked over to the book. "An ancient history book about Old Magic!" Harriet exclaimed. She proceeded to read aloud.

66 After the Tuatha Dé Danann defeated Dagda mór at the second battle of Moy Tura, Lir expected to receive the kingship. However, the kingship was granted to Bodb Dearg, leaving Lir enraged.

To placate Lir, King Bodb Dearg offered his eldest daughter to Lir in marriage. Their marriage was happy, but she died after having four children.

Bodb Dearg sent his other daughter, Aoife, to marry Lir. Aoife had a reputation, for she was known to use dark powers. Aoife became jealous that Lir lavished all his time upon his four children.

Aoife took the four children of Lir to swim in the lake. She used her dark magic and turned them into swans.

When the children of Lir transformed into swans, their voices remained, and so Lir discovered the truth. He used magic to turn Aoife into a spirit of the air, and she was never again seen.

Her spell kept them swans for 900 years.

I was struck speechless. How was Harriet reading a book of ancient magic? How did she know what Old Magic was?

I looked at Edison. He appeared to be thinking the same thing.

"A, a Polyglot!" he muttered, and then promptly fainted.

CHAPTER 11

"Quick, Harriet, help Edison to the chair."
Harriet and I dragged Edison over to a chair and struggled to get him up on it.

"Slap him across the face hard," JenniFur said.

"That's not very helpful," I muttered.

"I'm doing my best," Harriet said.

"I was talking to the cat."

"That's what they do in movies." JenniFur jumped onto Edison's lap, stood on her hind legs, and tapped his face with her paw. When there was no response, she peered into his face.

Edison awoke at that moment and screamed.

"What is it?" I asked him.

"Oh, it was only JenniFur's face," he said with relief.

"I told you I'd fix him." Her tone was altogether too smug.

"What's a Polyglot?" I asked him.

"A polyglot is somebody who can read several languages."

"I know that, but I expect you are talking about a Seelie Polyglot?"

Edison rubbed his forehead. "Yes, that's right. Did I faint?"

"Yes. It was the shock of seeing Harriet."

"It wasn't my fault!" Harriet protested.

"I think we'll need to go into the living room and talk about what's going on over some cake," I said. "Harriet, you take one of Edison's arms and I'll take the other."

"Will there be wine?" JenniFur asked.

"Yes, but none for you," I said.

JenniFur hissed a few rude words and ran out of the room.

"I'm all right. I'm all right," Edison said again, but he did allow us to lead him out of the secret room and into the living room, where I deposited him onto the Chesterfield.

"I'll start the fire," I said. I put some kindling

in the fire and threw a few firestarter cubes under the kindling for good measure, before topping it with some small logs. I stuffed some newspaper next to the firestarter cubes and set it alight. Soon, the fire was burning nicely.

"Now, will somebody tell me what's going on?"

"Are we going to have cake first?" Harriet asked.

"Oh, sure, I forgot. Edison, would you like some wine?"

Edison said that he would, and I left the room to fetch the cupcakes in the fridge. I brought them out, still in their cardboard tray, and stuck them in the middle of the coffee table. I wasn't going to stand on ceremony when I wanted answers.

I returned to the kitchen and fetched a small bottle of lemonade and a bottle of wine, two wine glasses, and one glass. Somehow, I managed to carry them all to the living room without dropping them. I handed Harriet the glass and a small bottle of lemonade, but she chose to drink from the bottle. I poured some wine into Edison's glass and into my glass and wasted no time taking a large gulp.

"Help yourselves to the cakes," I said, but it

seemed Edison and Harriet had already eaten two each. I selected a triple chocolate cupcake and ate it.

"Now, Edison, please explain everything to me. And don't forget, I don't know a lot."

Edison pointed at Harriet. "She's a Polyglot."

I sighed. "Yes, I got that, but exactly what is it? And I mean in Seelie terms."

Edison clutched at his throat. "Polyglots aren't supposed to exist anymore. They were supposed to have died out centuries ago. It must be a Night Court thing, because I haven't heard of any in the Summer Court, not for centuries."

I turned to Harriet. "Harriet, did you know you're a Polyglot?"

She seemed affronted by my question. "Of course, I did! I'm not a child. I'm not an idiot."

"So, you know you're a Seelie of the Night Court?"

"Obviously! Duh!"

I rubbed my temples hard and drained half of my wine.

Edison took over the questioning. "So, who else knows you're a Polyglot?"

"My parents and Uncle Caspian. He's a Polyglot too."

Edison gasped, and I was worried he would faint again. "Edison, are you all right?"

"Yes, no, yes, but Nell, don't you know what this means?"

"That Caspian can read lots of ancient languages too?" I said with a shrug.

"That's why he was kidnapped! So he could read the stolen book."

Harriet jumped to her feet. "What stolen book? What's happened to my uncle?"

Edison and I exchanged glances.

"Oops, he said too much," JenniFur said. "You humans can't hold your drink."

"You can hardly talk," I reminded her.

"I'm not a human any more, in case you hadn't noticed. I hold my drink better than most cats."

"That's probably true," I conceded.

"You need to tell me what's going on!" Harriet said, her face growing redder by the minute. "You tried to keep the fact that you were all Seelie from me. It's obvious you're a Bookmarker because you can speak to JenniFur, and she's obviously Seelie too. And Edison, you're obviously Seelie, and so are Daphne and Delilah. All you Summer Court Seelies stick together!"

"I think we should tell her," I said. "I think it would be safer."

Edison appeared to be hesitating, so I took the initiative. "We had a book, a book of Old Magic spells."

Harriet gasped. "Old Magic spells!" She appeared horror-stricken, and I wondered if I should be telling her all this, after all.

Nevertheless, I pushed on. "We think somebody by the name of Emerson Mortcombe was murdered. He borrowed the book from us, and the book was stolen. That was a short time before your uncle disappeared."

Harriet spoke more calmly this time. "So, the murderer kidnapped my uncle to make him translate the book."

Edison and I both nodded. "Yes, it would seem that is the case," Edison said slowly, "but who could possibly know your uncle is a Polyglot?"

"I don't know. I just got to town."

"That's just it, isn't it?" I said. "The sixty-million-dollar question. Somehow, the murderer knew that Caspian was a Polyglot, and so they have kidnapped him to make him translate the spells."

"And he hasn't translated the spells yet, because I haven't felt any Old Magic, apart from Emerson's murder and that little burst of it," Emerson said.

Harriet gasped. "You're a Hierophant! They're so rare."

"Nowhere near as rare as a Polyglot, it seems," I said. "Harriet, you can't tell a single soul that you're a polyglot as it could put you in terrible danger."

"Apart from Daphne and Delilah, of course," Edison said.

"But Nell said not to tell anybody," Harriet protested.

"They will need to be in on it to keep you safe," Edison countered.

Harriet shrugged and popped another cupcake into her mouth. I reached for my wine, only to see JenniFur's head in my glass. "JenniFur!" I said.

Her head was stuck firmly, and it took me a while to extract her head from the glass.

"I couldn't drink much out of that glass," JenniFur complained. "It's a weird narrow shape." She hiccupped.

I poured myself some more wine and put my hand over the top of the wine glass.

"Is there more?" Harriet asked, after draining the last of her lemonade. "You need to tell me everything to make sure I'm safe."

"We have three suspects," Edison said. "Nora Beckett, Emerson's cleaning lady."

"Emerson was the murdered man, right?"

Edison nodded at her. "And then there was the doctor, Dr Logan Tate, who attended the death and said it was natural causes."

Harriet nodded. "If he's not Seelie, he wouldn't have known it was Old Magic."

"That's right," Edison said. "And the only other suspect we have is Algerone Riverty. Nell questioned Nora Beckett, and we both briefly spoke with Dr Logan Tate, but we are yet to investigate Algerone Riverty."

"I will help," Harriet said firmly.

I shook my finger at her. "Harriet, you would be in terrible danger if anybody discovered you were a Polyglot too."

"But how would anybody ever find out?" Her tone was belligerent.

"Somebody found out your uncle is a Polyglot and kidnapped him," I pointed out. "Whoever kidnapped him probably had no idea you were staying with him, and we have to keep it that way. If they know you're his niece, they might think you could be a Polyglot as well."

Edison agreed with me. "It isn't worth taking any chances. But how could anyone possibly know Detective Cole was a Polyglot? He didn't tell any of us."

"But you, Daphne, and Delilah aren't particular friends of his," I said. Edison shot me a pointed look, so I added, "And I only met him recently."

Edison nodded. "Point taken."

"I wonder if Emerson knew?" I asked him.

Edison shook his head. "Surely not, because he would have asked for Detective Cole's help to translate the book."

"There was a phone call the other day," Harriet said. "Uncle Caspian was having an argument with somebody. It wasn't a screaming type of argument with lots of swear words or anything like that," she clarified. "But my uncle seemed quite angry."

"Do you know what the phone call was about?" I asked her.

She looked up at the ceiling and rubbed her

cheek. "Let me think. Uncle Caspian said it was too dangerous, and it was best not to translate something."

I gasped. "But that fits! That would explain how the murderer found out. The murderer might've looked through Emerson's phone messages from the time he had the book."

"But the house cleaner or somebody else might have been there at the time," Edison said. "Was this the day before your uncle disappeared, Harriet?"

She nodded.

"Yes, it must be Nora Beckett, after all," I said. "She might have overheard the conversation then checked to see who Emerson had called. Harriet, did he say anything else, anything at all?"

"No, I don't think so. I could hear them both because the other man was yelling. Uncle Caspian was outside on the garden seat, and the window was open. He probably didn't know I could hear everything. I wasn't listening though, but I couldn't help it." She sounded defensive.

"Go on," I said encouragingly.

"This won't be a help because it was nothing to do with it, but the other man yelled and then he said he had to go because his football friend had just arrived."

"Then maybe Algerone did overhear the conversation too," Edison said. "It seems to be between Nora Beckett and Algerone Riverty. Both of them could have overheard the conversation."

I planted my palm on my forehead. "How silly of me! Nora said a doctor had come to the house. She was annoyed that Emerson told her not to disturb him, but the doctor was able to disturb him. I think I did mention it to you, Edison."

"So, we're back right where we started from," Edison lamented. "All three of our suspects possibly overheard the conversation between Emerson and Detective Cole."

"And Harriet, you have to be very careful," I added. "If the murderer discovers that you're Detective Cole's niece, then they could kidnap you to make him talk."

Harriet did not seem worried. In fact, she seemed excited by the prospect of being kidnapped. "They'll starve you and keep you away from your games," I added for good measure.

Now, Harriet looked truly frightened.

CHAPTER 12

"*I*'m bored." Harriet scratched JenniFur under the chin. "Can I go chuck some rocks at someone?"

"Sure," I replied, resting my head in my hands. We still had no idea where Detective Caspian Cole was, and I worried about him. I worried about his strong, strapping shoulders and his smile. And also his safety. I worried about his safety.

"After I chuck some rocks at someone, I was thinking of buying a six pack of beer," Harriet added.

"Great. Have fun."

"And I was going to drink it while I smoked a pack of cigarettes."

"It's always nice to have hobbies."

"Nell." Harriet thumped a book on the table in front of me. We were hanging out at my bookstore, while I tried to think of all the people who might have kidnapped Caspian.

"Huh?" I sat up.

"Rocks. Beer. Cigarettes."

"Right," I said, finally thinking about what Harriet had said. "All of those things are bad. All right, we need to think of something to do."

"No," Harriet said with a twinkle in her eye. "We need to think of the most likely suspect to investigate."

I rubbed my chin. "We've already investigated Nora Beckett and, to a lesser degree, Dr Tate. Who did you have in mind?"

Harriet reached into the pocket of her yellow raincoat—a raincoat I suspect she stole from Paddington the Bear—and pulled out four tickets. "Algerone Riverty."

"We haven't investigated him yet. He used to attend the footy with Emerson Mortcombe."

Harriet nodded. "Edison told me that the pair always sat in the VIP seats at Metricon Stadium, so I used my uncle's credit card to buy us tickets. His friend supports one of the teams playing today. I thought Daphne and Delilah could come with us too, just because they seem to need the socialisation."

"They're not kids, Harriet."

"They act like it. At least, Delilah does."

I took the tickets. The game was that night. Luckily, Metricon Stadium was on the Gold Coast, which was just down the mountain. "These tickets were seventy-five dollars each!" I exclaimed. Caspian was going to kill me when he checked his credit card account—if he checked his credit card account. If he wasn't already…

Harriet's voice snapped me out of my reverie. "Algerone might know something about the victim. He might know something about where my uncle is, Nell."

"So, we just follow him?"

"Yep. We see if he talks to anyone. We see if he does anything strange. It's a long shot, but we need to investigate each suspect in turn, and you haven't investigated him yet, have you?"

"No." I considered there was nothing else to do at the moment, and Harriet really was bored. She needed the distraction, too. We both needed the distraction.

"Okay," I said.

Harriet squealed. "Yes. Thank you!"

"I don't know what you hope to find out by observing a suspect at a football game, though."

"I've given it a lot of thought," Harriet said. "Algerone might have stolen the book to sell it for a fortune to somebody else. If that's the case, it would be wise for him to meet the buyer or his fence somewhere other than the mountain. A crowded footy game would be as good a place as any, I guess. A place he could go to without arousing suspicion, but a place he could disappear into a throng of people."

I was impressed. "Wow, you *have* given it a lot of thought."

An hour later, we were on our way to Metricon Stadium. The Gold Coast Suns were playing, which made sense since Metricon Stadium is their home ground, and so were the Geelong Cats, a team not made up of cats but of people.

"I should sue," JenniFur had replied when I had told her about the Geelong Cats. "That's feline appropriation."

"That's not a thing," I had told her, and then I hurried out of the house, because you never ever want to disagree with a cat.

"I'm bored," Harriet said in the car. She tapped her fingers against her knee. "Are we there yet?"

"No."

"Are we there yet?"

"No."

"Are we—"

"Harriet, no we are not!" I said, and I tried to sound very stern.

"Well," Delilah said, poking her head into the front seat. "Are we there yet?"

"Why don't we put on some music?" I said.

"Excellent," Daphne replied. "I prepared a playlist for this very use."

It turns out Daphne had brought along a CD called "Music for Elevators," which is how we ended up listening to music they play in elevators for forty minutes as we drove to Metricon. I would have preferred to hear Harriet ask if we were there repeatedly, but I didn't want to turn off the CD as Daphne seemed to be having some sort of spiritual awakening to it, and her eyes had glazed over.

Thankfully, the car ride ended, and I managed to find a park at the train station. We caught a shuttle bus from the train station to

Metricon, which only took five minutes, and soon we were all sitting in our seats. The VIP seats were fancier than I felt comfortable with—instead of a metal fence in front of the first row, there was a fence of glass, which meant you didn't miss a moment of the action. The local team, the Suns, had boxes on the ground which shot up sparks as the team ran out.

In Australian Rules Football—or footy as we all call it—each team has a song. A fight song, if you will. The song is played when the team runs out onto the ground, and when the game is over, whoever wins has their song played over the speakers. The team then goes into their locker rooms, where they gather in a circle and sing the song. I wondered if any other sport in the world had songs. I knew there were chants, and some of those chants in some of the places in the world could be crude, but no one really chanted anything but the team name in Australia.

Footy was a bit like Quidditch, except there was no Golden Snitch, no broomsticks, and no wizards or witches. So maybe it wasn't like Quidditch at all. Yet the goal was to score more points than the opposition. There were four posts at either end of the ground. If you kicked the ball between the middle post, you got six points, but if you hit the post or kicked the ball between the side posts, you only got one point. It was Australia's way of saying, "You had a go, and we respect that, so even though you failed, we will give you a pity point."

"I'm bored," Harriet said, snapping me to attention. "Sport is so boring. I don't even know who we are cheering for, Nell."

"You bought the tickets," I said.

"Because I want to spy. Have you seen Algerone yet?"

"No," I said. "Yes!"

I spotted him in the front row. He was a slim, balding man with a small nose and huge glasses that made him look like a bug. I wish I'd brought my glasses. The players looked like ants, and I had no idea what was going on, because I couldn't see anything.

"He's not meeting with anyone," Delilah said.

"Not yet," Daphne muttered.

"Go and flirt with him." Harriet elbowed me in the ribs.

"Why me?"

"You and Algerone are both a million years old," Harriet replied.

I felt my heart stop. Surely, I didn't look the same age as Algerone? He seemed old enough to be my father. I tried not to feel personally offended, and I failed.

"I don't know how to flirt," I muttered.

"It's easy," Daphne said.

We all looked at her, stunned. Daphne didn't seem the type to indulge in anything as frivolous as flirting.

Daphne nodded. "Indeed. I once seduced the Count of Monte Cristo with nothing but a crystal bikini and a fan. It was no easy feat, and yet I triumphed."

"I left my crystal bikini at home," I replied, "so that's a shame."

"I'll flirt with him," Delilah said. "Unlike my sister, I don't need a fan to attract a man's attention."

She stood, rather dramatically, and then strode towards Algerone. Soon, she was sitting in the seat beside him. She put her hand on his knee and laughed at everything he said. I hadn't lied earlier. I was terrible at flirting. I didn't know how to pretend unfunny men were funny. It wasn't a skill I ever wanted to learn, but if I did, I probably wouldn't ask Delilah for tips.

After five or so minutes, another man who was carrying two beers joined Algerone. He handed one beer to Algerone, at which point Delilah returned to us.

"They've made plans to go to the pub after the game," she said.

"Did you find out anything else about his friend?" I asked her.

She nodded. "Yes, he lives in Southport, and they're going to a Southport pub. Algerone is going to stay there the night because he'll be drinking."

"I wonder if his friend is the buyer or the fence," Harriet said.

Daphne frowned. "Maybe he's just a friend."

"I'm hungry. Is there anything to eat?"

Delilah laughed. "Come on, Harriet. We'll go and grab some food."

After they left, we took our seats. Algerone looked behind him, I assumed to see where Delilah had gone, but waved to somebody.

I turned to find out who, and saw a short, slim man in an oversized jacket. Algerone at once left his seat and approached the man. They walked over to the wall, and both were acting in a furtive manner.

I stood and edged my way over to them. I needed to get closer so I could hear what they were saying. When they saw me, they both left the seating area with considerable speed.

CHAPTER 13

I pulled Daphne aside. "Algerone is going to the pub with his friend directly after the game," I said. "We need to leave the game a little early. I'll take you all home, and then I'll go back to his house and search it."

"Not a break and enter!" Daphne clamped both her hands over her eyes.

I hurried to reassure her. "No, nothing like that. I'll just skirt around the outside of the building and look in the windows. I'll call out for Caspian, that is, unless Algerone has close neighbours."

"It sounds too dangerous to me," Daphne said. "What if he comes home early?"

"He's made definite arrangements to go to

the pub and then home with his friend," I said. "Even if I only search his place for half an hour, that will give me plenty of time if he changes his mind and goes home. And that's highly unlikely."

"Then I should come with you," Daphne said. "Edison and Delilah can mind Harriet."

I had been hoping she would volunteer. "Thanks, that would be wonderful," I said with enthusiasm.

The game started, and soon the crowd was vocal. Algerone returned, minus the furtive man, and sat next to his friend in the front row.

I looked around for the furtive man but didn't see him anywhere. I continued to watch Algerone, but he didn't do anything out of the ordinary. He didn't do anything suspicious at all.

At quarter time, I walked around the aisles of the VIP seating section, looking for the man. There was no sign of him anywhere. I walked inside to the bar areas and searched. Again, there was no sign.

It wasn't a terribly big place, so I should have seen him. He must have had a ticket because people weren't allowed in without tickets. Did he pay seventy-five dollars just for a brief meeting with Algerone? There could be no other explanation. The question was, why?

I searched on my phone for Algerone's address but came up blank. I texted Edison and told him about our plan and asked if he happened to know where Algerone lived.

Edison got back to me fifteen minutes later and, to my relief, supplied Algerone's address.

The second quarter had started, so I searched for the address on the maps app on my phone. It didn't take long to locate the house in a somewhat remote area across from paddocks and on the edge of town. That would certainly be a good place to hide a kidnapping victim.

My excitement grew. Would I be able to find Caspian that very night? It seemed too much to hope for.

Yet, if Algerone had kidnapped Caspian, would he stay overnight at Southport with a friend? At first, I thought not, but then considered that he would need to go about his usual routine so as not to throw any suspicion onto himself.

At half-time, Harriet was complaining that she was bored. "But I thought you wanted to come here to spy on Algerone," I said.

"We've been spying on him all this time, and

he hasn't done anything," she countered. "I don't think anything is going to happen for the rest of the night."

I wasn't so sure, but then again, I was keen to snoop around his house. "All right then, we'll leave now."

We crossed the road and walked to the shuttle bus. I was relieved that we weren't the only ones leaving the grounds, and although the shuttle bus didn't have many passengers, it took us back to the train station. From there, it was easy to find our way back to the road and then back to the M1.

"You're back early," JenniFur said. "Just in time for my dinner."

I was certain Edison had already fed her, but I fed her again, just to keep her happy. It wasn't a good idea to make a cat unhappy.

Edison walked out of the kitchen. "You're really not going to go through with this plan, are you?"

"It will be perfectly safe. Algerone is staying in Southport overnight with his friend because he's drinking," I said.

He nodded. "I saw that in your text. Nell, if Algerone is the murderer, he might have security measures around his house. Are you willing to take the risk?"

"Yes," I said firmly. "Even if he gets a security alert that somebody is snooping around his house, I'll be gone by the time he gets back, and if he's the murderer, he's not likely to call the police."

"I agree with Nell," Daphne said, surprising me. "This investigation is going nowhere. We have to take it to the next level."

Edison frowned so hard that his brows met in the middle. "All right, but make sure you take your phones and call at the first sign of trouble."

"Hopefully, there won't *be* any sign of trouble," I said.

"If you see anything suspicious, get out of there fast," Edison persisted.

"Sure. I wonder if I can find something to disguise my appearance."

"Just wear dark clothes and something to cover your hair," Edison said.

"Okay, I'll be right back." I had only gone a few paces when Daphne said she'd go home and find something suitable to wear.

By the time I came back down the stairs, dressed in black track pants, a black sweater, and a black beanie, Daphne was already standing there and dressed in similar clothes.

"Snap," JenniFur said. "Nobody would know who you are. You both look like a couple of indiscriminate blobs."

"Thanks," I muttered.

"What did JenniFur say?" Daphne asked me.

"She said we looked nice."

"I did not!" JenniFur said. "I said you looked like a couple of horrible blobs."

I ignored her. "We had better go," I said.

As we hurried out the door, Delilah said to me, "I have some gloves, and I brought an extra pair for you and a torch each."

I thanked her. A sense of trepidation hit me. I hadn't even thought about torches. I truly was unprepared, but then again, this was an unexpected opportunity to search Algerone's house.

"Do you know the way?" Daphne asked me when we were halfway there.

"Yes, it's on the edge of town, on the Beaudesert side. It looked like a fairly isolated spot on the map app."

"I certainly hope it is," Daphne said. "If not, we won't be able to do any snooping."

"We'll cross that bridge when we come to it," I said.

I was relieved to see the area did, in fact, appear to be fairly isolated. As I turned into Algerone's street, I didn't see a single house, but I did see a long driveway stretching right back.

I stopped outside a high brick fence. "I can't see a number."

"I see it! It's partially obscured behind that hedge. Thirty-four."

"That's it!"

"Kill the lights," Daphne said.

"It's a long driveway to the house, as far as I can tell," I protested. "How will I see?"

"The moon is bright enough for you to be able to see the road if you go slowly," Daphne said, "and it's not as if there's a sheer drop over the edge of the driveway. You don't want anybody seeing a car going up the driveway and reporting it to Algerone."

"They'll simply think it's Algerone coming home." Still, I did as she asked. I turned off the lights and edged forward. It wasn't so bad after all, at least not at the speed I was driving. When I reached the front of the house, Delilah said, "Drive around the house and park there."

"I certainly hope Algerone doesn't come home. I thought we'd be able to park down the street from his house and walk to snoop around. Now, my car is trapped here, and if he comes home, he'll know we're up to no good. We won't be able to think up a reasonable excuse."

"You saw how much he was drinking at the game, and it was only the first half," Daphne said. "Plus, his plans were to go out drinking with his friend. There would be only one chance in a million that he'd come home tonight."

"I certainly hope you're right. But what about torches? The neighbours will think it's suspicious if they see lights flashing around the house."

"Not necessarily," Daphne said. "They might just think Algerone was at home."

I broke out in a cold sweat. "Okay, let's get this over with."

I hurried over to the house, with Daphne behind me. "You go to the left, and I'll go to the right. We'll meet at the front door," Daphne said.

I hurried away, my fear tempered by the fact I was hoping to find Caspian. I shone my torch in the first window. To my surprise, the curtains were not drawn, and I was able to see inside. It was a kitchen. I moved onto the next room, which was a bedroom. Once more, the curtains were not drawn. It looked like any other bedroom. I continued on until I met Daphne at the front door. "None of the curtains were drawn," I said. "He doesn't seem to be hiding anything."

Daphne waved her finger at me. "That is precisely what somebody would do if they *were* hiding something." She tried the front door, but it was locked.

"Do you know how to pick locks?" I asked her.

She didn't answer but hurried off to the left. I followed her. She tried the back door, and to my surprise, it was open. "It's open!" I exclaimed.

"People often don't lock their doors in the country," she said. "Come inside. and we'll have a good snoop around. Whatever you do, don't take off your gloves." With that, she turned on a light.

I gasped with horror. "Daphne! Why did you turn on the light?"

"Because it won't seem at all suspicious," she said. "Nobody finds house lights suspicious, but they might find torch lights inside the house suspicious."

I had to admit she had a point, and it was

certainly easier to search with the lights on. "What should we search first?"

"You take the living room, and I'll take his bedroom."

"Sure." The living room was fairly sparse. There was a big chest of drawers, on top of which was perched a large TV. Every drawer was filled to the brim with all manner of paperwork, mostly faded receipts, some many years old.

I searched through them as quickly as I could, and then turned my attention to the large chest that served as a coffee table. There was a coffee mug sitting on it alongside a box of pizza. I opened the lid and saw several old pizza slices still inside. "Eww," I said.

I carefully removed the cup and the pizza box from the chest and looked inside. There was nothing of any note.

Against one wall stood a walnut credenza complete with a marble top. I looked inside it, but it had a collection of old ornaments. I figured Algerone had inherited them, possibly from his mother.

At that point, Daphne emerged from the bedroom. "There are huge posters of Brisbane Lions and Fitzroy players from back in the day and framed signed guernseys in there. Did you find anything?" she asked me.

"Not a thing. I came up blank. You?"

She shook her head.

"We should call out for Caspian now. The neighbours won't hear us."

She said that was a good idea. "You call out for him, and I'll look on the floors to see if there's maybe a trapdoor to a basement where he could be keeping Detective Cole."

I didn't need telling twice. "Caspian! Caspian!" I called, hurrying through the house. I looked under every bed, calling Caspian's name as I went.

I was thoroughly discouraged by the time I returned to the living room. "There's no sign of Caspian, or the book, or anything to suggest Algerone is the murderer or even Seelie," I said.

"And all the floors are timber, so it's easy to see if there are any trapdoors," Daphne said. "The only outbuilding I saw was the garage. Let's look inside it."

She turned off the light, and we hurried out of the back door and headed to the garage. We slipped in by the creaky side door, and once more, Daphne turned on the light.

The garage was absolutely crammed full. There was no room for a car. Several lawnmowers in various states of disrepair sat in the middle of the garage. Yellowing pages tumbled out of cardboard cartons. An old green couch sat against one wall, covered with various types of saws and other tools.

"We can't take this at face value," Daphne said. "Let's have a quick look around here, and watch out for redback spiders."

I shuddered. I walked forward and promptly fell over something. I picked myself up, bit back the rude word I was about to say, and rubbed my shin. "Ouch!" I said finally. "I'm glad there aren't any close neighbours as they would have heard all those paint cans fall on the concrete floor."

"Caspian!" Daphne shrieked.

My blood ran cold. "What is it?" I asked urgently.

Daphne turned to face me. "I thought we should call out to Caspian here as well."

My stomach churned. I thought something had happened. "Oh, sure."

Daphne continued to call out to Caspian, while I walked around the garage looking for anything incriminating. "I doubt he would keep a rare book here because it's absolutely full of dust," I said.

"Maybe he told that secretive man at the game where it was, and he's gone to fetch it," Daphne suggested.

I shrugged. "Maybe. Or maybe it was all innocent."

My spirits fell. We'd had a golden opportunity to search Algerone's house and garage. If Algerone was the murderer and kidnapper, then surely we would have found something.

Where was Caspian? And was he okay?

I was sick to my stomach.

CHAPTER 14

The situation of Emerson's heirs remained unresolved. We didn't even know if he had any heirs. Dr Tate seemed to think he didn't, and he was in charge of the Wild Lime Mountain community page collection for the funeral. Still, we wanted to be certain.

Edison had asked his friend, the lawyer Alfred Denison, for information about Emerson's heirs and the terms of the will, but he refused to give out any information whatsoever. For this reason, Edison had decided we had to break into the lawyer's office to find out for ourselves.

"You don't need to worry. He doesn't have a security system, not that I could see anyway,"

Edison said brightly as I drove in the direction of the lawyer's office late at night.

"Can you be one hundred percent certain?" I asked him. "I don't particularly want to end up in prison."

"If he does, it isn't a back-to-base one," Edison said. "I did have a good look around. Besides, what does he have to guard? He doesn't have any big clients."

"I hope you're right," Daphne muttered. "This could all go south."

"Really, what could go wrong?" Edison asked.

"Don't say that!" Delilah shrieked. "When people say that, something always *does* go wrong."

"Don't be so superstitious," Daphne scolded her.

"I do hope Harriet is all right," I said. "I worry that I left her alone."

"She's in our house, not yours," Daphne said. "And don't forget, we *do* have a security system there. And JenniFur is looking after her."

"Harriet is only a young teenager," I said. "I'm terrified she will do something silly, like leave the house."

Delilah chuckled. "Not after we downloaded

those games for her. I think she'll still be glued to the TV when we get back."

We had reached the lawyer's office, and Edison directed me to drive down a little dirt track. "The car won't be seen from the road here," he said. "Turn around so you can be facing in the right direction, just in case we have to make a fast getaway."

"I'm not going to be involved in a high-speed car chase!" I said in horror.

"If you are, you had better let me drive," Daphne said.

Both Edison and Delilah yelled, "No!"

It was hard for me to turn the car around on the narrow track, but I finally managed without getting bogged.

"Now, let's put on our beanies," Edison said. We were all dressed in tight-fitting dark clothes, and we pulled the beanies on our heads. I hoped this would be more productive than our recent foray into breaking and entering. On the off chance that Alfred did have security cameras, it would be harder to recognise us, or so Edison had said. However, his beanie did nothing to disguise his long white beard.

We crept through the bushes and emerged behind the building.

"Alfred is quite absent-minded, so he might have left a door or a window open," Edison said.

"What if he hasn't?" I whispered.

"Think positive," Delilah said. "We'll cross that bridge when we come to it—*if* we come to it."

"I'll pry a window open if I have to," Edison said.

I didn't want to break into a lawyer's office, but I was desperate to find Caspian. Time was of the essence. I had to discover the murderer and then find where the murderer was keeping Caspian. I was relieved that Edison hadn't felt another burst of Old Magic. That meant Caspian was refusing to translate the book. I figured the murderer would keep Caspian alive, at least until that book was translated.

"Wait behind the building," Edison said. "I'll go alone to the door and try it."

I stood there, shivering in the cool night air, adrenaline rushing through me. It seemed an age before Edison returned. "Unfortunately, it's locked," he said. "Let's try these windows."

We tried the windows in the building, but they

all appeared to be locked. "It looks like you'll have to smash a window, Edison," Delilah said.

"Not so fast." Daphne rattled the window. "These are old sash windows, and this one hasn't been latched properly. I think I can get it open."

She continued to wriggle the window and finally, it opened. "Maybe you should go in first, Edison, since it was your idea."

Edison seemed quite happy to be the first to break and enter, but he got stuck halfway through the window. Daphne grabbed his legs and pushed them hard. He fell on the floor with a thud. "Ouch!"

"Be quiet," Daphne hissed. "Burglars don't make any noise."

Daphne pushed Delilah through the window, and then I pushed Daphne through the window. That meant I was left alone on the other side of the window. I looked around for something to stand on and found a plastic crate. I picked it up and carried it to the window, but when I stood on it, my legs went through it. "Maybe I shouldn't eat so many cupcakes," I lamented, checking my legs for scratches.

After much huffing and grunting, and with help from Edison and Daphne, I managed to get through, although I also landed heavily on the floor. I was sure I would have plenty of bruises later. I was already looking forward to a long, hot bath and a glass of wine, and the adventure had only just started.

"I wonder why he left the lights on," I asked.

Delilah chuckled. "You know, I hadn't even noticed that!"

"Maybe for security reasons," Edison offered.

Delilah continued to chuckle. "Well, it certainly hasn't helped. We all climbed in."

"Where should we start looking?" I asked Edison.

"I'll look on his desk, and you three search through the filing cabinets," Edison said.

There were three filing cabinets, so we took one each. "The files are not in alphabetical order," I lamented.

"I suspected that, which is why I suggested we should all come," Edison said. "Otherwise, only one or two of us would have sufficed."

"Have you found anything yet?" Daphne asked him.

"No, but I'll tell you when I do. Oh look, Alfred has left his glasses here. He's as blind as a bat without them."

"Maybe he has another pair," Daphne said. "Otherwise, how would he have driven home?"

"He doesn't drive anymore," Edison told her. "He always gets a taxi."

I looked up from urgently thumbing through mismatched files. "His air conditioner is noisy."

Delilah agreed with me. "I think it sounds like it's broken. It sounds like a pig looking for something to eat in the bushes."

Then, to my abject horror, the large wingback chair in the corner of the room turned to face us. I bit back a scream.

"Who's there?" the figure in the chair said. It took me a moment to realise it was indeed the lawyer, Alfred Denison.

He stretched and yawned. I could only assume he had fallen asleep.

I wondered what to do. Should we all jump out of the window, run for the car, and hightail it out of there?

Edison grabbed Alfred's glasses and put them in his pocket.

Daphne stepped forward. "You're having a dream," she told him. "I am the ghost of Christmas Past." She gestured to Delilah. "This is the ghost of Christmas Present, and this one is the ghost of the Christmas Yet-to-come."

"I'm dreaming?" Alfred asked.

"Yes," Daphne said firmly.

"But aren't there four of you? Who's that other one?"

"That's Ebenezer Scrooge," Delilah told him.

Alfred scratched his head. "But the ghosts of Christmas appeared to Ebenezer Scrooge. Why am I dreaming about you and seeing Ebenezer Scrooge as well?"

"Because it's a dream," Delilah told him.

"Aha." Alfred smiled and nodded.

I was glad it made sense to him, because it certainly didn't make any sense to me. Still, I was happy that he was swallowing this whole bizarre story.

His next words dashed my hopes. "But it's not Christmas!" He frowned deeply.

"But it's winter," Delilah said, "and in the northern hemisphere, it's winter at Christmas. We can't be everywhere, you know."

Daphne elbowed her hard in the ribs, but Alfred appeared satisfied by her explanation. If he wasn't, he didn't voice his concerns.

"What do you want with me?"

We all looked at each other. Daphne was the first to speak. "We are visiting you so you can help us with Emerson Mortcombe."

"But he's dead! He died only the other day."

"We know that," Delilah said. "We're spirits, after all. We need you to tell us who his heirs were. Who will inherit his house?"

Alfred rubbed his eyes. "This dream seems so real."

"Answer our question and you can go back to sleep, and maybe dream about cats."

Alfred smiled. "Emerson didn't have any heirs. His will left everything to the classics department at the University where he was a lecturer many years ago."

"Then who is the executor of the will?"

"I am."

"And who will pay for his funeral and his service? Was there a provision for that left in the will?"

Alfred shook his head. "No, there wasn't, but Dr Tate kindly came to see me after Emerson died and asked me if there were any heirs. He offered to help raise money for his funeral."

"Then he will be blessed," Delilah said. In

lowered tones, she whispered to me, "That is, if he isn't the murderer."

"I didn't know I left the window open," Alfred said. "Did I do that in my dream?"

I hurried to shut it. "We should leave now," I whispered to Edison.

"Continue with your dream," Edison said, slowly and in a monotone, as he set Alfred's glasses back on his desk. "Shut your eyes and do your best to go back to sleep. Have pleasant dreams, and thank you for assisting the ghosts of Christmas Past, Present, and What-is-yet-to-come."

"You're welcome," Alfred said. His head dropped back and once more, the loud snoring sound emanated from him.

I grabbed Edison's arm. "The front door," I said. We hurried to the front door. Thankfully, it had the type of latch that could be locked and then pulled firmly shut from the other side.

We all sprinted to my car. I got there first. I jumped inside, shaking. "I can't believe he was still in his office," I said when the others climbed in the car. "Do you think he'll be all right?"

"Maybe he sleeps there a lot," Edison said. "It was warm in there, at any rate. At least we found out for certain that Emerson didn't have any heirs."

I drove back to my apartment. "But how does that help us in our investigation?" I asked him.

"I don't know, to be honest," he admitted. "Maybe we'll discover something at the funeral."

"Like what?" My question was met with silence.

I was disheartened. We were no closer to discovering the identity of the murderer or to finding out where Caspian was. For all I knew, he could be imprisoned in a cold, dank cell—or worse.

CHAPTER 15

I'd had another sleepless night. Time was running out, but as hard as I tried, I was no further to solving the murder or Caspian's disappearance.

"You look grouchy," were JenniFur's first words when I stumbled into the kitchen.

"I…" I began, but she interrupted me. "I'm hungry. Feed me now!"

"You're always hungry," I muttered. I poured some food into her bowl. I turned on the coffee machine and stared at it, willing it to heat up faster.

It wasn't long before Edison arrived. "Are we opening the shop today?" he asked me.

"We'll have to, I suppose, but we still need to investigate."

"Harriet and I can mind the store, and you can investigate."

"But we're all out of suspects," I said. "What's the next step?"

Edison stroked his beard. "Well, I was thinking. It seems strange to me that nobody saw Detective Cole being abducted. Even if they didn't see anything that was suspicious though, maybe somebody saw *something*."

"You'd think so." I shrugged.

"Why don't you go to his neighbours and ask them if they saw anything that day?"

"That's a good idea," I said. I half suspected Edison wanted me out of the shop so I wouldn't pace up and down and stress, but it was a good idea, nonetheless.

"Is Harriet awake yet?"

I shook my head. "If she was, she'd be playing games."

"Enough of the inconsequential chitchat," JenniFur said. "I'm starving."

"There's still some food left in your bowl," I told her.

JenniFur fixed me with a glare. "Your point?"

I knew better than to argue with a cat. I poured some more food into her bowl, and she ate it while purring loudly.

I waited until just before nine before driving to Caspian's street. I assumed the police had questioned the neighbours, but I didn't think Detective Stevens had been as thorough as I would be. After all, he hadn't taken Caspian's disappearance seriously at first.

I started with the house next door to Caspian's. There was a sign on the door asking people not to knock, but I couldn't see a doorbell. With no other option, I called out, "Hello?"

A woman about Delilah and Daphne's age stuck her head around the door. I must not have looked threatening because she opened the door all the way, then stepped onto the porch before shutting the door behind her. "I can't let the cat out," she explained.

"I'm Nell Darling. I own the bookstore in town."

She smiled and nodded.

"I don't know if you're aware, but Detective Caspian Cole is missing."

She nodded. "A nice detective asked me

questions about that, but I told him I didn't know anything."

I nodded. "I was in his house with his niece on Monday morning just after eight when he disappeared. He said he was going to the car to fetch something, but then he never returned."

"How strange."

I agreed. "So, you didn't see anything at all?"

She shook her head. I pressed on. "Did you hear anything?"

"No. I was in my garden around that time, and I thought I would have seen something. I did see you arrive and another man leave."

"That would have been Edison, the bookstore manager," I told her. "Detective Cole went missing only about five minutes or so after that."

She scratched her head. "That's very strange. I think I would have been out in the garden at that time."

"Did you happen to see a car in the street that you hadn't seen before? I mean, anything at all, even if it seems entirely inconsequential, could be a help."

She scratched her brow. "No, I didn't see anything out of the ordinary. Isn't that strange! I was trying to fix my hydrangeas. They're not doing well, you see. Why, the ones at the nursery just up the road always look wonderful, but when I buy them and bring them home, they don't do well. I give them plenty of water, and as you would know, the soil here is wonderful. I don't know what I'm doing wrong with my hydrangeas."

"Is it the colour that you don't like?" I didn't know much about hydrangeas, only that you could change the colour with certain minerals.

"No, not at all. They don't even flower. They look quite dead. Come, I'll show you." She led me to a patch of garden with a collection of stalks. "That's them," she said sadly.

"How strange," I said. "The rest of your garden is beautiful and flourishing. Maybe the ones at the nursery were straight out of a greenhouse or something like that."

She seemed to brighten a little. "Yes, that must be it."

I looked over to where Caspian's car was still parked. The hydrangea garden afforded a wonderful view of the area. "Is this where you were when you saw me arrive and Edison leave?"

She nodded. "I was planting some daffodil

bulbs in this garden bed, as I've all but given up on the hydrangeas."

"That's strange because you can easily see his car from here."

She agreed. "I did have my head down from time to time, but I should have seen somebody being kidnapped."

"Well, thank you for your time. Good luck with the hydrangeas."

She smiled and gave me a little wave.

I walked to the house on the other side of Caspian's house. A tall, thin man was out in the garden. He greeted me warmly. I at once introduced myself. "Hi, I'm Nell Darling, the owner of the local book shop. I'm a friend of Caspian's next door."

He straightened up and dropped his gardening trowel in his wheelbarrow. "Oh, that's a terrible thing! A detective came here asking if I saw anything the other day. What day was it again?"

"Monday morning, about eight," I said.

He nodded. "I always have my breakfast on the porch here." He indicated two white wrought iron chairs with an intricate design of ivy and a little white table between them. "Yes, I always have my tea and toast outside about that time."

"And you didn't see anything?"

"I saw a man leave and then Caspian arrive with a lady. No, it was the other way around. Caspian arrived with a lady, and then the man left. The lady looked a little like you."

"It *was* me," I said. "He went missing only ten or so minutes after that."

"And you haven't heard from him?"

I shook my head. "He's officially a missing person."

"Oh dear. That's terrible."

"He went to his car to fetch something and didn't come back. His phone was found under the car. Somebody abducted him. Did you see anything?"

He shook his head. "No."

"After the other man left, did you see Caspian go out to his car?"

He shook his head again.

"How long were you sitting on the porch?"

"Probably until nine or so."

"And you didn't see a stranger in the street, or a car you're not used to seeing, or hear a noise at all?"

"No, nothing. The last thing I noticed was the man leaving."

"So, you were sitting out here the whole time?"

He nodded. "Yes, I was reading the paper."

"When Caspian was abducted, he dropped a bottle of wine, and it smashed on the road. Did you hear anything like a wine bottle smashing?"

"No, and I do have very good hearing. I heard you calling out for Caspian loudly."

My spirits fell. "Thanks for your time."

"I hope he turns up soon."

I shot the man a smile. "Thanks. So do I."

I made my way back up along his raised driveway. Both neighbours on either side of Caspian's house were outside at the time Caspian was abducted, but they saw nothing.

How was that possible?

I walked to the house directly across from Caspian's house. It was on a hill and had a good view of the road and of the front of Caspian's house.

I knocked on the door and then rang the doorbell for good measure, but nobody was home. I was halfway back to the front fence when a woman called to me. "Can I help you?"

She was hurrying down the path to me, clutching a pair of big green garden gloves.

I walked back to her. Once more, I introduced myself and went through the whole story.

The lady, who introduced herself as Emily, was quite dismayed about Caspian's disappearance. "Like I told the detective, it was very strange that I didn't see him," she said. "I saw you arrive. It was you, wasn't it?"

"Yes, it was me," I said, remembering for the first time that day that I had been wearing rollers in my hair, pyjamas, and giant fluffy slippers.

"I saw another man driving away. I saw you come out and call for Caspian quite loudly."

"But you didn't see what happened in between times?" I asked her.

"No, and I told the detective that was strange. I put in a row of magnolias there." She indicated a row of young saplings. "And even though we've had a bit of rain recently, I was watering them in well. Magnolias like a lot of water."

I found that quite strange—not that magnolias like a lot of water, but that she saw two separate events and not what happened in between, namely, Caspian's abduction. "So, you were watering the magnolias when you saw the man

181

leave, and then you were still watering them when you saw me come outside and call for Caspian?"

She seemed a little embarrassed. "While I'm not a busybody, you understand, it *is* awfully boring watering plants. I tend to daydream or watch what's going on around me."

"Oh yes, that's perfectly understandable," I said. "Thanks for the information."

"I'm sorry I couldn't have been any more help."

I walked to every house in the street. Some people weren't home, but those who were had heard nothing. They hadn't heard anything untoward or seen anything untoward. They had not seen a stranger in the street or even a strange car in the street.

I was beginning to think something otherworldly was going on.

CHAPTER 16

I hurried back to the bookshop. Edison was finishing up with a customer. When she left, I asked him, "Where is Harriet?"

"She and JenniFur are in your apartment. I keep checking on her from time to time, but I thought it's best that she's not seen in public."

"But I took her to a football game," I said.

"I meant not seen here on Wild Lime Mountain with us," Edison said. "How did you go?"

I told him everything that had happened. "And what's even stranger," I said, "you saw what I looked like that day when I arrived at Detective Cole's house."

Edison chuckled. I glared at him and

continued, "But all three of his closest neighbours recognised me when I spoke with them today, even though I looked completely different now. Yet, they didn't see Caspian abducted."

Edison narrowed his eyes and stared off at the ceiling.

I pushed on. "One or two of them saw me go out and call for Caspian, and they saw me arrive, but they didn't see him abducted, which happened in between me arriving and me calling out for Caspian. And the lady opposite who was watering her garden said she was in the yard the whole time. Edison, do you think somebody used Old Magic to conceal the abduction?"

Edison shook his head. "It is strange, to be sure, but that would have taken a lot of Old Magic, and I would have felt it."

"What then? There must be something magic or otherwise supernatural involved. All three people could see the road outside Caspian's house, but not one person saw him abducted or saw anything out of the ordinary."

"There's something in the back of my mind, but I can't quite figure out what it is," Edison told me. "Never mind. I'm sure it will come to me at some point. Nell, why don't you ask Emerson's neighbours if they saw anything? The police haven't checked with any of those neighbours because they don't know it was a murder."

I clasped my hands. "That's a great idea! Of course, the police wouldn't have asked around. I can tell the neighbours that someone stole my book."

Edison nodded encouragingly. "Well then, off you go. It's not a big customer day today, possibly as it's raining heavily down on the coast."

"It might be heading this way," I told him. "When I arrived in Caspian's street, the sky was clear, but clouds are gathering now."

I walked towards the door and then walked back again. "Oh, I don't even know Emerson's address!"

Edison wrote it on a piece of paper and handed it to me. "Don't take any chances, Nell. At the first sign of trouble, come straight back here."

His words alarmed me. "Do you think there'll be trouble?"

Edison shook his head. "No, not at all, but better to be safe than sorry."

Emerson's street branched off another street in the southern part of town. When I arrived there, I was dismayed, because there were only houses on one side of the street. On the other side of the street was a steep hill covered with trees and shrubs. Emerson's house was not overlooked like Caspian's was.

My spirits fell. There was even less chance here of somebody seeing something, but then again, the street was narrow and one-way, so a strange car was more likely to be noticed.

There was nowhere safe to park on the street, given it was so narrow, so I parked in Emerson's driveway. The neighbour on the boundary fence was pruning his roses.

"Are you looking for Emerson?" he began in gloomy tones, no doubt thinking he would have to break the solemn news to me.

I at once put his mind at rest. "No, I know he passed away on Monday morning."

The man breathed a sigh of relief. For what seemed to be the umpteenth time that day, I introduced myself. "I'm Nell Darling and I own the book shop in town. Emerson borrowed an old rare book from me, but nobody knows where it is."

"I don't have a key to his house, but his lawyer might."

I shook my head. "Thanks, but my bookstore

manager was the one who discovered the body. He looked for my book but couldn't find it. It's old and extremely valuable. We think it might have been stolen." In case he thought I was accusing him of theft, I hurried to add, "On Monday morning, did you see any strangers in the street, or any strange cars?"

"No, I didn't."

"Did you hear anything, anything at all?"

He shook his head.

"Maybe his cleaning lady, Nora Beckett, saw something. Do you remember if she was there the day that he died?"

"No, but she was there the day before. Or maybe it was the day before that. I can't quite remember. And that doctor was there too." He took off his hat and scratched his head.

"And no one was here on Monday morning?"

"No, nobody at all."

"Were you inside the house or outside the house then?" I was worried about asking too many questions, but he didn't seem to mind.

"I was painting my fence," he said, indicating the white picket fence at the front of the house.

"It's lovely," I said. "I've always wanted a picket fence."

"I can give you the name of the builder, if you like," he offered.

"Thank you, but I live in an apartment above my bookstore, so I don't have anywhere to put a fence."

His face fell. "That's a shame."

I agreed. "It is. Do you remember what time you started painting the fence?"

"It was just before seven in the morning," he said. "They forecast rain for the afternoon, and I thought I heard some thunder in the distance. I wanted to get the first coat on as soon as possible, so I started quite early."

"And when did you finish painting?"

"About nine or so. Actually, I'm not sure, but I stopped painting when the doctor came over to tell me that Emerson had passed away in his sleep."

I nodded. "And did you go inside your house at any time?"

He shook his head. "No, I was in a hurry to finish before the storm came. It was only the first coat, so I wasn't worried about a few sprinkles of rain on it, but it wouldn't have been good if it had been completely drenched."

"Thanks so much. Sorry to ask you so many

questions. It's just that the book is very valuable, and I don't know what's happened to it."

"I don't mind at all," he said with a smile. "It's nice to chat. Emerson wasn't one to chat. He always had his nose in a book."

"Do you mind if I look behind Emerson's house, to see if a thief could have had access over the back?"

"None of my business!" he exclaimed. "Feel free! I hope you find who stole your book."

I walked down behind Emerson's house. There was a high, chain-link fence along the rear, with an unkempt hedge in front of it. I stuck my head through a gap in the hedge and saw a house directly behind Emerson's.

If somebody had gained access to Emerson's house without the neighbour seeing, then they would have had to go through the house's yard. As I was watching, two large dogs ran at me, barking ferociously.

I hurried back to the neighbour who was still pruning his roses. "I figured that since you didn't see anybody, the thief must have gained access to Emerson's house from the house directly behind it, but there are two big dogs."

He chuckled. "Oh, nobody could get past

those dogs. They are outside dogs too, so it wasn't as if they could have been asleep inside the house."

The dogs were still barking. "Did you hear those dogs barking on the morning of Emerson's death?"

He frowned for a moment before answering. "No, I don't believe I did. I can't be sure, mind you, but once they get set off barking, they don't stop for hours. It always irritates me, and I don't remember being irritated that morning."

"Thanks so much for your help," I said.

I walked to the neighbour on the other side of Emerson's house. "Are you selling something?" a voice said.

I jumped and looked around for the source. It was an elderly lady sitting in a white bamboo chair, leaning over and spray-painting plant pots bright red.

"No, I'm asking Emerson's neighbours if they saw anything the morning he died." So as not to alarm her, I quickly added, "He borrowed a valuable book from my bookstore, and it's gone missing. I think perhaps somebody might have stolen it."

She stood up. "Do you like this colour?"

"I do indeed," I said.

She beamed from ear to ear.

"Were you home the morning Emerson died?" I asked her.

"Yes, I was painting those pots over there." She pointed to a row of bright turquoise plant pots.

"I love that colour too," I told her. "I'm asking Emerson's neighbours if they saw anyone strange, or maybe a car they didn't know, the morning that he died."

She wiped a hand over her face, leaving a stripe of bright red paint. I wondered if I should mention it to her, but given that her hands were covered in paint, I thought that maybe she didn't mind.

"I only saw the doctor and a man with him. They both came to tell me that Emerson had passed away in his sleep. So sad."

"It certainly is," I said. "There was nobody around before that?"

"Not that I noticed," she said. "George was out painting his picket fence. Maybe you could ask him if he saw anybody."

"I did, and he didn't see anyone either. I was wondering if somebody could maybe get around to the back of Emerson's house and slip in unnoticed?"

She chuckled. "Do you hear that noise?" She cupped her hand to her ear.

"You mean the barking?"

"Yes. Once something sets off those dogs, they bark for hours. Nobody could get past them. They're completely ferocious."

I thanked her and left. This was exactly the same situation as at Caspian's house. Now, I was firmly convinced something was out of the ordinary.

CHAPTER 17

"*And* it was exactly the same with Emerson's neighbours as it was with Caspian's neighbours," I concluded.

"Strange, very strange indeed." Edison tapped his fingers on the countertop. "As strange as it sounds, somebody managed to abduct Caspian, slipped into Emerson's house to murder him and steal the book, and nobody noticed anything."

"This will sound really strange, but do any Seelies have the power of invisibility?" I asked him, followed quickly by, "Don't laugh!"

"I'm not laughing at all," Edison said. "It's a perfectly reasonable question, but the answer is no. Besides, even if the person who abducted

Caspian was invisible, Caspian certainly wasn't, but nobody saw him."

"It's a puzzle, that's for sure," I said.

"What's a puzzle?" JenniFur asked me.

"You were sitting right there. Weren't you listening?"

"I'm a cat," she said. "We only listen when it benefits us."

I took a deep breath and let it out slowly, before repeating everything I had told Edison. When I looked up, JenniFur was asleep.

"That was a waste of my breath," I said to Edison.

"What was a waste of breath?"

I spun around. Harriet was standing there. "What happened?" she asked me.

I told her everything I had told Edison and JenniFur.

"There must be a logical explanation," Harriet said. "That's what my father always says."

"I'm certain there is, but what is it?" I threw both hands up to the ceiling.

"And Harriet has a little secret she neglected to tell us," Edison told me.

"It wasn't a secret," Harriet said. "I just didn't tell anyone, that's all."

JenniFur awoke and said, "Humans! Honestly!"

Before I could ask, Edison told me. "It's Harriet's birthday today!"

"I didn't know that. Happy birthday, Harriet! How old are you?"

"Fourteen."

"And she wasn't going to tell us," Edison said. "Her father called to wish her a happy birthday. I was right there, so I couldn't help but overhear."

"It's not a big deal," Harriet said with a pout.

"We'll have to have a birthday party for you," I said.

Harriet continued to pout. "I'm too old for a birthday party."

"No, you're not," I told her. "I still have birthday parties."

Harriet raised her eyebrows. "You do? And you're so old!"

"Thanks." I frowned at her.

"Daphne and Delilah are excited about Harriet's birthday party," Edison told me. "Well, Delilah is particularly excited. They're making a birthday cake and bringing it over for the party."

"I refuse to play games," Harriet said.

"What? But you love games."

She rolled her eyes. "I love video games. I refuse to play stupid party games like pin the tail on the donkey."

"We won't have any party games," I promised. "There'll just be birthday cake and lots of party food."

Harriet's mood improved considerably.

"And presents," Edison added.

Harriet's mood went up another notch.

"I'll go find her a nice dead rat," JenniFur said. "She'll love that. I'll try to find one that's partly decomposed." With that, she jumped out of the window.

"So, when are we having this party?" I asked Edison.

"Tonight, after the funeral today."

I gasped. "The funeral is today?"

"Didn't I tell you?"

"No, you didn't."

"I only found out in the last hour or so. It's at midday in the community hall. It's a memorial service rather than a funeral as such. There will be no graveside attendance or anything like that."

"If the murderer attends…" I began, but Edison interrupted me.

"It seems certain that the murderer will attend. They always do."

"Then I was going to ask if you would sense any vestiges of Old Magic from the murderer?"

"I doubt it, because I haven't felt any since that little burst," Edison said. "Still, I'm certainly going to try."

"What do you hope to find out at the funeral?"

Edison shrugged. "I have no idea, to be honest. But we're going anyway, so we might as well be on the alert. Our three suspects will most likely attend."

I ran my hand over my eyes. "It's a pity we didn't have one suspect over the others, because I could go to that suspect's house and snoop around, to look for Caspian."

"Maybe we should do that anyway," Harriet said. "We can break into their houses and look for my uncle."

I agreed with her. "I'm thinking that's not such a bad idea, although breaking into Algerone's house was unproductive."

Edison waved his finger at us. "It's not safe. The perpetrator uses Old Magic. They might be expecting us, and who knows what manner of tricks would be lying in wait for us. You have no idea of the power of Old Magic. I, for one, would not want to come up against it."

I wondered why he hadn't protested so strongly when Daphne and I had snooped around Algerone's house. Still, he had no idea we were going inside. "But you're a Hierophant, Edison. If there was some sort of booby-trap or warding spell, you would sense it."

"Yes, possibly."

"Are we going to do more breaking and entering?" said a voice from behind me.

I spun around to see Delilah. Daphne was standing behind her, looking entirely exasperated. "What's all this about?" Delilah asked us.

I was tired of telling everybody the same thing over and over again, so I left Edison to explain.

Daphne pursed her lips. "It sounds dangerous."

Delilah disagreed. "It sounds like fun, and Edison will sense any magic."

"Maybe we should do it as a last resort," Edison said, "but today, we'll need to go to the funeral."

"I made you a nice hat for the funeral," Delilah said to Harriet. She was clutching a large pink, red, and white striped bag which she unzipped and from it produced with a flourish a tinfoil hat, complete with party sparklers and sequins.

"It's a combo birthday funeral hat!" Delilah said. "You can wear it for your birthday party tonight too. I put black sequins on it to make it fitting for a funeral. Even better, aliens won't be able to mind-control you, Harriet."

Daphne muttered some very rude words.

Harriet appeared horror-stricken. "Err, thanks," she said, staring wildly at the hat. She took two steps backwards.

"I don't think it's safe for Harriet to go to the funeral," I told them. "We can't have the murderer catch on that Harriet is Caspian's niece, as the murderer might try to abduct her too. We've already been over this."

"Yes, I've decided I don't want to go to the funeral," Harriet said, still eyeing the hat with askance. "I'll stay here with JenniFur."

"I think somebody, a human, should stay with Harriet," I said.

This time, Harriet did not protest.

We all looked at each other. After a lengthy interval, Daphne sighed. "I'll stay."

Harriet grabbed the tinfoil hat and went back to the living room, presumably to play games.

Seconds later, she emitted a bloodcurdling scream.

CHAPTER 18

We all rushed into the living room. I half expected somebody would be dragging a protesting Harriet out of the window.

However, she was standing there, her mouth open in a continual, loud scream, and she was pointing to something on the ground.

"I've never had anybody so excited over a gift before," JenniFur said, looking entirely pleased with herself.

"It's a rat!" Edison exclaimed.

"Not just any rat—a long dead, half decomposed rat," JenniFur said with pride. "Isn't the smell delightful! Just what any girl would want for her fourteenth birthday. She will never forget that."

"That's for sure," I said. "Harriet, JenniFur says that rat is your birthday gift."

Edison quickly removed the rat from the room.

"Quick, stop him!" JenniFur screamed. "He's trying to steal Harriet's rat and eat it."

"It was a gift for me?" Harriet asked. At least she had stopped screaming.

"Yes, sometimes JenniFur likes to give rats to people as gifts," I explained. "She is a cat, after all. She was especially delighted to find this particular rat for you."

Harriet forced a smile. "Oh, thanks. That's, err, nice of you, JenniFur."

"But don't worry, we won't give you rats as gifts," Delilah said.

Daphne rolled her eyes. "Obviously!"

I hurried around, checking all the windows, so JenniFur couldn't fetch another rat. I looked to see if she was offended, but she had curled up in a comfortable chair and had fallen asleep.

Edison returned to the room. "I've put the rat in a safe place for Harriet," he said with a big wink.

"Thank you, but JenniFur has fallen asleep."

Edison heaved a huge sigh of relief.

When we walked out of the room, leaving Harriet to her games, we discussed Harriet's gifts in whispered tones.

"What does a girl of that age want?" Daphne asked. They all looked at me.

I shrugged. "It's a long time since my daughter was fourteen. I don't have a clue, to be honest. I know she likes games."

"Surely, we shouldn't encourage her to indulge in such unseemly activities," Daphne said, a terse expression on her face.

"But we're not her parents, and she won't be staying here for long," I pointed out. "She will be going back to Caspian's, once we find him."

If we find him, I silently added. Knots once more formed in my stomach. Where was he? And was he okay? I decided the answer to the latter must be no—nobody would be okay if they were kidnapped.

Edison patted my shoulder. "Maybe we'll find out something of use at the memorial service."

I didn't know what to expect from the service. Edison told me repeatedly that the murderer would be there, but I didn't know how that could help.

When Edison, Delilah, and I arrived at the funeral, I was surprised at the number of people milling around outside the community hall. I drove past it, looking for somewhere to park.

"There was a big collection taken up on the community Facebook page," Edison told us.

"That was good of everybody," I said. We got out of the car, and I locked it, and then we walked up the slight rise to the building.

Everybody turned to stare, and I realised Delilah was wearing Harriet's combo birthday funeral hat. I had been so preoccupied with thinking about Caspian's kidnapper that I hadn't even noticed. "Oh, you're wearing Harriet's hat," I said without thinking.

Delilah smiled and nodded. "I asked her if I could borrow it, and she said she didn't mind at all. What a thoughtful girl."

"Indeed," I said.

We walked into the building, Edison and Delilah greeting various people on the way. I briefly spoke with some of my regular customers.

Once inside the building, Edison directed us

to sit at the back of the building. "We can see everything from here," he said.

"But what benefit will that be?" I asked him. "It's not as though the murderer will throw themselves on Emerson's coffin and make a public confession."

"But his coffin won't be here, will it?" Delilah asked, apparently confused.

"I was speaking in general terms," I said.

Delilah continued to look confused.

"But detectives always attend funerals of murder victims," Edison said. "There's a reason that they do that."

"Maybe it's for the free food afterwards," Delilah said, smiling and nodding as she spoke. "Police officers are very fond of doughnuts. They are always eating them on TV."

Edison and I exchanged glances. "Maybe the murderer will give something away," he said.

I sighed. "I only wish we could have broken into each suspect's house while they were here at the funeral service."

"It's a good idea, but we would have needed more time to prepare."

"I think you're right, Edison," Delilah said.

"But it's certainly something we should look into doing, and sooner rather than later."

People had been filing into the building as we were speaking, and now Dr Tate walked up the stairs to the stage. "Welcome everybody, and thank you for coming," he said. "Thank you all for your generous contributions. We have now raised enough money for a plot and a headstone plus engraving at the local cemetery."

Delilah cheered loudly. Everybody turned to look at her.

"And now, anybody who wishes may come up and talk about Emerson. I'll go first. He was a lovely person, a good friend."

"I didn't know they were friends," Edison whispered to us.

"They must have been," Delilah said, "because he's organised everything for the funeral."

The doctor was still talking. He extolled a list of Emerson's virtues, either real or imagined, at great length and in flowery language. When he finished, Delilah clapped loudly. This time, nobody turned around to look at her, but a polite round of clapping did go up around the room.

"Has anyone seen the other two suspects?" I asked.

"There's Algerone Riverty." Edison pointed to a man covered in football gear. He was wearing a Brisbane Lions signed guernsey, a Brisbane Lions beanie, and a Brisbane Lions scarf.

Delilah tut-tutted. "Oh, my goodness! That's hardly something appropriate to wear to a funeral service."

You can hardly talk, I thought, amused, looking at her brightly coloured tinfoil hat complete with antennae. Aloud, I said, "And where is Nora Beckett?"

"Down there." Edison pointed to the front row, over to my right.

"I'd love to be able to search her house right now," I said. "And the doctor's as well."

"You and me both," Edison said, "but it would be too dangerous to do it without careful preparation."

I sat there, my stomach churning, listening to people speak about Emerson. Or rather, I wasn't listening—I was wondering what to do next. The three suspects were not giving anything away, and what's more, not one suspect stood out amongst the others.

I was at a complete loss.

The service seemed to drag on forever, and then Doctor Tate took the stage once more. "We have booked a room at the café next door, the back room, for refreshments. It's all free, but please leave a coin donation at the door."

"If you have to make a donation, then it's not free," Delilah said rather loudly. This time, the people in several rows turned to look at her. She smiled and waved to them.

"After all that, we didn't find out anything," I lamented to Edison. "It was just as I feared."

"Maybe we'll find out something at the café," Edison said. "Keep your eye on the suspects."

"What exactly are we looking for?" I asked him.

"We'll watch to see if they speak to anyone in particular or maybe to each other."

"Do you think two or more people were in it together?"

Edison shrugged. "Anything is a possibility."

An eerie, rumbling sound drew my attention, at once unnerving me. Was it an earthquake? Or was something evil brewing?

CHAPTER 19

I grabbed Delilah's arm. "Can you hear that awful noise?"

"Um, it was just my stomach rumbling."

JenniFur's head peeked over the top of Delilah's large handbag. "No, it's me. I'm a spy."

I gasped. "JenniFur! Cats aren't allowed at funeral services or in cafés."

"That's disgraceful. That attitude is a blot upon society," JenniFur said with a growl.

"Quick, pop your head back down so nobody can see you." To Delilah, I said, "Why on earth did you bring JenniFur?"

"She jumped into my handbag. She gave me a significant look, so I realised she wanted to come along as a spy," Delilah said in reasonable tones.

"Besides, Daphne was minding Harriet, so I knew JenniFur didn't need to mind Harriet as well. I thought it was a good idea. I can put my handbag down near one of the suspects, and JenniFur can report to you everything they say."

"That would be a good idea, but only if the murderer is involved with somebody else."

"What do you mean?" Delilah asked me.

"I mean, the murderer isn't likely to utter a confession. This plan would only be of use if the murderer says something incriminating to somebody else."

"Then how do you know the murderer won't?" Delilah said brightly.

"She's right," JenniFur said from inside the handbag. "Will there be wine at the café? Or maybe champagne?"

"There won't be anything of the sort," I told her. "And there won't be cat food either."

"I'll settle for cake."

"Delilah, please take JenniFur home at once, and then come straight back."

Both Delilah and JenniFur sighed.

Everyone by now had left the building, so I walked behind the others into the café next door.

I hadn't been to that café before. Well, I had gone once, and that was why I hadn't gone again. The barista had given me a cold latte, and when I had asked her simply to heat it in the microwave, she had been quite rude to me and refused to heat it. Consequently, I had never gone back to that café.

The back room of the café was large, a long narrow rectangle. The walls were painted black, and paintings by local artists covered most of the walls. There was a long table in the middle of the room, or rather, several long tables pushed together.

Edison charged ahead of us and sat opposite Nora Beckett, who was sitting with a scowl on her face. We were in luck, because Algerone Riverty was sitting only two people away from her. There was no sign of the doctor.

When Delilah came back, Algerone's face lit up. "Hello again," he said with a big wink. "Imagine seeing you again, so soon!"

Delilah winked back.

I wondered what I could say to engage the suspects in conversation, in the hopes they would incriminate themselves. I came up blank.

Nora had her head down, sipping something,

tea or coffee. I couldn't tell because it was in a Styrofoam cup.

"Hello again, Nora," I said.

"Hello." She looked at me from under her brows. I fancied she looked like a troll hiding under a bridge. She certainly had the same attitude.

"These are my friends, Edison and Delilah," I told her.

"Hello," she said again.

"You knew Emerson, didn't you?" Delilah said.

"Yes." She bent over her cup.

Well, that wasn't going well. Once more, I tried to think of something to say, and once more came up blank.

Just then, the man sitting next to Delilah made a strange, strangled sound.

"I think he's choking on a peanut!" Algerone said. "Quick, somebody help him!"

Delilah jumped to her feet, grabbed the man around the middle, and squeezed. He made an even more horrible sound, and the next thing I knew, Nora Beckett clutched her face and fell to the ground.

"Thank you, thank you ever so much," the

man who was choking said to Delilah. "I swallowed a peanut the wrong way."

I didn't have time to ponder how anybody could choke on something as small as a peanut—after all, I was certainly no medical expert—when people rushed to Nora's aid.

A man helped her back to her chair. "What happened?" he asked her.

She let out a string of obscenities. When I sifted through all the obscenities, I realised she was saying that the choking victim's peanut had hit her in the eye.

Dr Tate pushed his way through the crowd. "Let me see that eye," he said to Nora.

Nora whimpered, covering her eye with both hands.

"Come on, let me see. You might need treatment," Dr Tate said in an authoritative tone.

He managed to pry Nora's fingers away from her eye. After peering into her face for an interval, he said, "It doesn't look as though it's done any damage. You're very lucky. The way you screamed, I thought you had an eye injury."

Nora let out another string of obscenities, grabbed her handbag, and hurried out of the cafe.

Dr Tate then turned his attention to Delilah. "Nobody uses the Heimlich manoeuvre these days," he said.

"But I just did," she protested. "And what's more, it worked."

"The recommendations have been changed," the doctor said. He took Delilah by the elbow and moved her to the side of the room. The two of them appeared to be deep in conversation.

"I felt the faintest tinge of Old Magic when we first walked into the room," Edison whispered to me.

"Has it gone?"

"No, it's still here."

"That means it isn't Nora," I said, "given that she just left."

Edison shook his head. "Not necessarily. Even if the person who caused it had left, the feeling of Old Magic would still hang around here for a little longer."

"So, you don't have any idea who it's associated with?" I asked him.

"No," he began, but Algerone interrupted him.

"How did you both know Emerson?"

Edison was the one who answered. "He often

borrowed books from the bookstore. This is Nell Darling who owns the bookstore."

Algerone shot me an appraising look. "You look familiar. You're new to town, aren't you?"

"Yes, that's right," I said. "Were you a good friend of Emerson's?"

"Oh yes, we went to all the games together at the Gabba and Metricon, if Brisbane was playing."

I already knew this, but I feigned interest. "You must have been a close friend, then."

He nodded vigorously, causing his beanie to fall over one eye. He pushed it back. "Yes, yes. He will be sorely missed."

"Emerson borrowed a very rare and valuable book from the bookstore a few days before he died," Edison told him. "It's missing."

"Missing?" Algerone repeated. "Did you look for it when you found him?"

"How did you know I was the one who found the body?" Edison asked him.

Algerone seemed surprised by the question. "Everybody in town knows."

"When you last visited him, did you happen to see a book?" I described the book and its dimensions.

"What was the book's name?" Algerone asked.

"I have no idea," I told him. "It was in an ancient language."

He nodded slowly. "Emerson loved those ancient languages."

"Did you see the book?" I persisted.

"Possibly. I'm not interested in books. No offence, you being a bookshop owner and all."

"None taken," I said. "It's strange that it's gone missing."

"I don't remember seeing a book like that, but he was always working on something. Have you asked Nora Beckett about the book? She only just left. She was Emerson's cleaning lady for years."

"I did, and she didn't see it either," I told him.

"What was the book about?"

I looked at Edison. "We don't really know, because we couldn't translate it," I said.

"Did Emerson translate any of it?"

"No," Edison said firmly. "He couldn't make head or tail of it."

"Maybe he called someone and asked for their help."

Edison appeared disinterested. He was certainly a good actor. "Maybe he did. He didn't tell me. Besides, I think it's one of those ancient languages that nobody has translated yet."

"There's a first time for everything," Algerone said. "Do you know anybody else who is able to translate ancient languages?"

Edison shook his head. "No, Emerson was the only person I knew."

A man I didn't know walked over and slapped Algerone on the back. "Hey! How's that fishing cabin of yours?"

"What, what?" Algerone sputtered. "Look, I'm in the middle of a conversation. I'll catch up with you later."

"You have a fishing cabin?" Edison asked. "Where is it?"

"Near Jacobs Well," the man supplied. "It's in a remote location. Great to get away from the wife." He laughed heartily. "When are you going to invite me again, Algerone?"

"I'll catch up with you later." Algerone was clearly trying to end the conversation.

Edison elbowed me in the ribs. Emerson and the man continued to talk, but I tuned out. I'd heard enough. I had an idea. I didn't know if it was an idea of any substance, but I needed to get back to the bookshop, to the secret room, and do some research.

Something was niggling at me, lurking just out of reach in the recesses of my mind. Sure, a cabin would be good place to hide Caspian, but something else had occurred to me. If only the idea was fully formed.

But first, there was Harriet's birthday.

CHAPTER 20

When we got home, Harriet and JenniFur were asleep on the couch. Daphne was drinking wine.

"JenniFur didn't get any of that wine, did she?" I asked her.

Daphne shook her head. "No, but she tried. What happened? Anything of interest? On second thoughts, tell us about it later. This is Harriet's birthday party!"

Birthdays were wonderful. Not for me, but for other people—birthdays were wonderful. There was cake, which went straight to my wobbly bits and made them even wobblier, and there were presents, which other people received but my ex-husband always forgot to buy for me. There were balloons, which stressed me out because they were dangerous to wildlife, and also candles, which stressed me out because of the fire hazard.

I didn't want to be a party pooper, however; it was Harriet's birthday, which meant I needed to be upbeat. I needed to be serene. I needed to find a present for a fourteen-year-old in the next hour before we got the party started. What did fourteen-year-olds even like these days? Marbles? Yo-yos? Jacks? No. Harriet had said no to games. Which meant I needed to buy her wine? No, she was too young for wine.

A cheese platter! I had always wanted a cheese platter! Well, not so much a cheese platter but a hostess gift where there was cheese, a wooden chopping board, a bottle of wine—I intended to substitute lemonade—and a cheese knife wrapped up in cellophane. I left Daphne and Delilah to set up for the party as I jumped in my car and drove to the local supermarket. Unfortunately, there were not enough items at the supermarket to make a hostess gift for Harriet, so I did have to settle for a cheese platter.

When I arrived home, I put the cheese platter on the table for gifts. Delilah had already finished the cake—it was of George Michael.

"Does Harriet even know who George Michael is, Delilah?" I asked, confused.

"Every fourteen-year-old girl I know has the biggest crush on George Michael," Delilah replied brightly.

"How many fourteen-year-old girls do you know?"

Delilah thought for a moment. "Just Harriet, I guess. But when I was younger, every girl loved him."

Daphne snorted rudely. "I doubt Harriet has ever heard of George Michael or Wham! She's going to hate that ridiculous cake."

"I'm sure it's fine," I replied, desperate to avoid another argument.

"It's not fine," Daphne said. "Thankfully, I am in touch with the youth of today, and I too made Harriet a birthday cake."

It was of Jon Bon Jovi.

"Er, great," I said. Suddenly, I felt terrible for buying Harriet a cheese platter. We really were about to throw her the worst birthday party of all time. I decided to buy her an online gift voucher to a gaming store.

"I'm here," Edison said, as he entered the bookshop with a gift and a cake he'd ordered from a bakery down the mountain. "Sorry, girls. I couldn't order from you because I wanted the cake to be a surprise for Harriet."

"I already made her a cake," Daphne said.

"So did I," Delilah replied.

"Well, yes," Edison said kindly. "But I thought we might all be a little out of touch with today's young folks, so I called my sister and asked what we should get our young friend, Harriet, for her birthday. Also, what Harriet might like on her cake."

"Give us a look then," I said, hoping it was better than George Michael and Jon Bon Jovi.

It was Michael Bolton. The third cake was decorated with the face of Michael Bolton.

"He's today's biggest heartthrob, according to my sister," Edison said.

"How old is your sister?" I asked, confused.

"Seventy-five."

There was a knock at the door. Edison answered it. "Harriet," he said when he returned, "a birthday card has arrived for you."

Harriet jumped up and grabbed the card. "It's from my dad! It's in his handwriting."

She ripped open the card and read for a minute.

"What does it say?" Delilah asked. "I love birthdays!"

"He wished me a happy birthday and said that there's a truck arriving with my present." Harriet dropped the card and ran over to the window. We all followed her.

There was a truck in the driveway, and the driver was unloading a miniature goat. *Well*, I thought, *that can't be for Harriet. It must be for one of the farms down the mountain*. But then the driver herded the goat over to the shop.

"Don't open the door!" I yelled.

It was too late. Harriet had opened the door, and in came the goat. Immediately, chaos rained down upon our heads. The goat at once nibbled on the books and the furniture. She then sat on Michael Bolton's cake face before moving on to eat Jon Bon Jovi. Daphne shrieked, and Edison put his hands over his ears.

"There must be a mistake," I called out.

"I asked for a boat," Harriet said with obvious dismay. "A boat! Not a goat!"

"You need to learn to enunciate," Edison yelled. The goat was eating his beard.

"I don't want the goat!" Harriet burst into tears.

"Can I have her?" Delilah asked. "I've always wanted a pet goat."

"You're not having a goat!" Daphne yelled at her.

Harriet stopped crying and shot Delilah a shrewd look. "I'll swap you the goat."

"What for?"

Harriet tapped her chin. "Let me see. Red Dead Redemption. Oh, and Red Dead Redemption II."

I held up my hand. "Wait! I'm checking this out first." I tapped away on my phone. "No, you're too young for it, Harriet."

"What else then?" Delilah asked, while Daphne tried to get the goat to release Edison's beard. "Money?"

"How much?"

"Fifty dollars."

"I can't buy a game for fifty dollars!"

"Well then, a hundred dollars."

Harriet pouted. "The goat is worth more than a hundred dollars!"

Delilah tut-tutted. "It's rude to refer to her as 'the goat.' What is her name?"

"Her name?" Harriet asked, clearly put out. "I don't think she has one."

"Why, that's terrible," Delilah said. "I think I will name her Butt-head."

"That's a ridiculous name," Harriet said, her tone filled with scorn.

Delilah frowned, but then added, "I know! I will name her Vincent van Goat!"

"But she's a girl," Harriet protested.

A terrible thought hit me. Where was JenniFur? In all the commotion, the adults had left their wine glasses unguarded. I left Delilah and Harriet arguing over the goat's name and over how much money she was worth, and went in search of JenniFur.

I found her, passed out on George Michael. It seems she had eaten half his face first.

"JenniFur!" I exclaimed.

She opened one eye. "The goat made me do it! With that, she fell back to sleep.

CHAPTER 21

*D*elilah tapped my shoulder. "Good news, Harriet and I have come to a financial agreement about Vincent van Goat."

Daphne appeared at her shoulder. "You're not keeping that goat!"

Delilah drew herself up to her full height. "I most certainly am! I will keep her in my side of the house. Now, enough talk about trivialities. Don't you want to find out what happened at the memorial service?

"Yes," Daphne snapped. "But you are keeping that goat in the paddock out the back, not in the house!" She sat down and picked up her wine. There wasn't much left, so she refilled her glass.

Delilah spoke up. "Algerone has a fishing cabin near Jacobs Well."

Daphne's mouth fell open. "Do tell! How did you find that out?"

"We nearly didn't find it out," Delilah told her. "Not long before we left, a man came up to Algerone and asked him how his cabin was. He said he'd like to be invited back again soon."

"That's right," Edison said. He had put the goat on a makeshift leash. "Algerone looked most put out about the man mentioning the cabin."

Daphne jumped to her feet, almost spilling her wine. "But that's it! Algerone is keeping Caspian in that cabin."

"I think something else is going on," I said. "It all hinges on the invisibility."

"What do you mean?" Daphne asked me.

"Nobody saw Caspian abducted. Nobody saw the murderer arrive at Emerson's or leave. Nobody saw anything, and this is in spite of the fact that there were neighbours outside and in the vicinity at the time."

Edison was clearly puzzled. "But we have discussed this before, Nell. Invisibility is not a Seelie power, and even if it was, the perpetrator wouldn't be able to make Caspian invisible as well."

I ran my hand over my eyes, most likely streaking my mascara, but at that point, I didn't care. "But don't you see?" I protested. "That has to be the key to everything. I've been so involved with trying to figure it out that I haven't had any cognitive space to think things through clearly."

"I do take your point," Edison said. "But where does that leave us?"

I shook my finger at him. "You know, there's something just sitting in the back of my mind that I need to remember. It's to do with something that wasn't as it seemed."

"What is it?" Delilah asked.

"Nell just said she couldn't remember what it was," Daphne said.

To forestall the inevitable argument, I asked Edison, "We haven't mentioned The Anvil and Reed lately. What do you know about them?"

"A terrible, evil organisation," Daphne spat.

"Daphne is right—for once," Delilah muttered. "They are evil."

"I already said that."

Delilah glared at her sister. "I was agreeing with you. You should be grateful."

"Edison?" I asked.

"Let me see. The Anvil and Reed was supposed to be around centuries ago, and then there is no record of them from Roman times until the Middle Ages."

"What did they do in the Middle Ages?" I asked him.

"I don't know of anything specific, given that they are such a clandestine and secretive group, but they caused havoc. They wanted to take over the world, that sort of thing."

Daphne nodded solemnly. "Yes, the old *world domination* thing. People try it every few centuries or so."

"And they used Old Magic then?"

Edison looked shocked. "Certainly not! There was no Old Magic used in the Middle Ages. No, Old Magic hasn't happened since ancient Irish times."

Now, I was thoroughly confused. "But wasn't Old Magic used to kill Emerson? And didn't you say there was a small burst of Old Magic after that?"

Edison waved one hand in the air. "Yes, of course. Let me explain. Old Magic hasn't been used from ancient Irish times until now."

"But nobody has translated that spell book." I protested.

"Not that one, but there must be others," Edison said. "Maybe not as detailed."

"Then let's get down to the nitty-gritties." I stared at each one in turn. "I don't think we've been thinking this through clearly. If the murderer killed Emerson with Old Magic, then clearly somebody had to translate that spell."

Edison stood up and waved his arms. "Of course!"

"What is it?" Daphne asked. "Have you figured something out?"

Edison sat down, and his face fell. "No, but what Nell said will lead us somewhere. I was in touch with my contacts in Wales and Ireland after Emerson's death, after I sensed the Old Magic, and they were shocked to hear about it."

"Did they have any information?" Delilah asked him.

"Hush, Delilah," Daphne said. "Edison would have told us if they had told him anything."

Edison looked shame-faced. "Actually, they did say something, but I couldn't see how it was relevant, so I didn't bother to mention it."

"What was it?" I prompted him.

"Just that there are rumours that they are amassing a register of every Seelie worldwide and every Seelie's power."

"But that seems impossible!" Daphne said. "Or at least, a huge undertaking that would take many years."

Edison readily agreed with her. "That's what I thought, so I didn't mention it. But my contacts said they started some years ago." He tapped himself on the side of the head. "I've been so foolish. Clearly, they found somebody who could translate a little bit of Old Magic."

"And that must be how they found out about Caspian too," I said. "He must have been on their register. But how did they find out about him?"

"Obviously, somebody is infiltrating Seelie," Edison said, "and Dingo Mountain has the biggest Seelie population of any town in Australia."

"Dingo Mountain?" I asked him. "I thought you said Wild Lime Mountain had."

Again, he tapped himself on the side of the head. "Silly me. It was called Dingo Mountain until just before you arrived in town, Nell. The government decided to change the name to Wild Lime Mountain, because it's a tourist town and they didn't want tourists to think wild dingoes were roaming around the area."

I nodded. "That makes sense. Okay, let's get back to basics. Somebody, the murderer, is helping compile the register of Seelie in Wild Lime Mountain. That person kidnapped Caspian and is trying to make him translate the book."

Edison nodded. "That's right."

I pushed on. "And whoever it is, was able to kidnap Caspian without anybody seeing. The murderer also arrived at Emerson's house and left without anybody seeing. That has to be a big clue."

"It does indeed," Delilah said, "but I just don't know what that clue could be."

Something occurred to me. "You were all surprised when you found out that Caspian and Harriet were Polyglots."

The three of them exchanged glances. "You could have knocked me down with a feather," Edison admitted. "I really didn't think there had been any for centuries."

"What other sorts of rare Seelies are there?"

Edison scratched his head. "I don't know. If you mentioned one, I could tell you whether it was a rare type or not."

"But I don't know any," I protested. "Do you have any textbooks on different types of Seelie?"

"I do, in the secret room."

"Then hurry along," Daphne said. "I think Nell might be onto something."

Harriet awoke and rubbed her eyes. "Could you all keep it down? Some people are trying to sleep."

"We think we're getting close to solving the case," I told her.

"Why, what's happened?"

"It's a long story which I won't bore you with, but we're going to look through books about the different types of Seelies to find ones that nobody thought existed anymore."

"Like me and my uncle," Harriet said proudly.

I nodded. "Exactly."

"I'll help."

"I'll help too," JenniFur said.

"But you can't read."

JenniFur appeared offended. "Of course, I can read! I just can't turn pages, that's all. I don't have opposable thumbs, if you hadn't noticed."

"What's JenniFur saying?" Harriet asked me.

"She wants to help."

At that moment Edison returned and set a pile of books on the table. "These are all similar books, and they should all have similar content," he said. He handed each one of us a book. JenniFur insisted he place a book in front of her and open it. I passed on her wishes.

"What are we looking for exactly?" Edison asked me.

"I know you said there isn't a Seelie power of invisibility, and even if there was, that they couldn't have made Caspian invisible too, but there must be something similar."

"We're looking for a Seelie who can make things around them, like what, turn invisible?" Harriet asked.

I nodded. "That's exactly what I'm looking for."

"I've never heard of such a Seelie," Delilah said.

"Well, if there is one, we will find it in these books." Edison opened his book, and the rest of us followed suit.

I was beginning to think we were on a wild goose chase. The book I was reading was particularly boring and taking a long time to get to the point. I shut it and reached for another book. It was far better. It had the name of the type of Seelie at the top of each page, followed by a description.

It was a thick book, and I had been reading for fifteen minutes when I let out a shriek. "I've got it!"

"You woke me up," JenniFur complained. She had fallen asleep on her book.

"It's a Concealer!"

Everybody looked at me. "I've never heard of that," Delilah said.

"A Concealer? What does it do?" Edison asked.

I consulted the book. "It says a Concealer is an ancient Seelie power that was thought to have died out in ancient Irish times, but there have been reports of one or two Concealers since the seventeenth century, according to the book," I told them.

"What exactly does a Concealer do?" Edison asked me. "What is the specific power of a Concealer?"

I was excited. "Pretty much what the name says. The book says that a Concealer can make things look different."

"I'm not sure I get your meaning," Delilah admitted.

"The book gives some examples," I said. "The first example is somebody stealing a loaf of bread from a table. The Concealer can hide the fact that they are going to the table, and they can also conceal the bread so that nobody sees the bread or the Concealer stealing it."

Edison nodded slowly. "I see. So, it's sort of like having the power of invisibility, only more far reaching."

"It is indeed more far reaching," I continued. "Another example is that somebody could make a room look different."

"Do you mean making a room look not shabby but luxurious?" Delilah asked me.

"No, not that," I told her, "although that would be possible too. Kind of the opposite. Somebody could be sitting in a room with lots of jewels around and hide the jewels from other people in the room."

"That makes sense," Delilah said.

I went cold all over. The solution that had been hiding in the recesses of my mind suddenly stuck me. "I know who the murderer is!"

"$\mathcal{W}$ho?" everybody screamed in unison.

"It's Nora Beckett." They all spoke at once, so I held up a hand for silence. "When I was at her house, I tripped over a metal chair, and it skidded along the floor. I was horrified, because I knew it would leave scratch marks on her floorboards. But when I looked around, there wasn't so much as a scratch."

"I'm not sure I understand," Delilah said.

"There would have been a scratch on the floor, only I couldn't see it," I explained.

Edison nodded slowly. "I see. You think Nora is a Concealer and that she had a Concealment on her house. It hid the scratch marks on the floor."

"That's exactly right," I said. "It's been bothering me ever since it happened. There was a terrible squeaking sound, and the air seemed to shimmer somewhat. I became a little dizzy. At first, I thought it was a migraine coming on, and then I thought I had eyestrain because I've been reading so much lately. It hasn't happened at any other time, but when I was in her house, things did seem to shimmer a little."

Edison took the book from me and read the entry. "Yes, it says those sensitive to Concealment might experience vision loss or dizziness when in the presence of a Concealment," he said.

I pushed on. "And at Emerson's memorial service, the man who was choking coughed up the peanut, and it hit Nora's eye. Dr Tate thought she should have an injured eye, no doubt as she screamed in pain, but when he examined her eye, he couldn't see anything wrong with it. That's what made me think something was wrong, that she was covering something."

"*Concealing* it," Delilah said.

I nodded. "Exactly. Maybe she's kept the Concealment on her house and on herself permanently. Well, at least for the moment, while all this is going on."

"But you didn't know about Concealers at that point, so why were you suspicious?" Edison asked me.

"No, I didn't know about Concealers," I admitted, "but I figured it all hinged on the fact that nobody saw anything. People were in their yards and should have seen something, but they didn't. I should have seen a scratch on the floor at Nora's house, but I didn't. Nora had an eye injury, and nobody saw it. It was only when she got the eye injury, and the doctor couldn't see anything wrong with it, that I began to think something was going on. Of course, I wasn't able to put the pieces together until I read all about Concealers just then."

"That's all well and good, but what are you going to do now?" JenniFur asked. "For all you knew, Nell, Caspian could have been sitting on a chair opposite you, and you wouldn't have been able to see or hear him."

My stomach twisted.

Edison looked up from the book. "It says the Concealment works on all Seelies except those who have shifted into other animals."

JenniFur jumped up onto the coffee table. "I can be the hero!" she said. "I can go to the Concealer's house and find Caspian."

"That's a great idea," I began, "but you would be in danger. Nora might suspect you're a Seelie who has turned herself into a cat, and she would likely try to do away with you."

"I'll snoop around and be careful. Maybe you should make me look like a stray. You could put some hair styling products on my coat and make my hair stand on end."

"You're far too fat to look like a stray," Harriet said.

"Thank you." JenniFur purred loudly. "Well, there goes that idea. Does anybody else have a brainwave?"

"We could lure Nora out of her house somehow," I said. "Wait, I have a better idea. She does work as a cleaning lady after all. Maybe we could wait until she goes to her next appointment."

"That's a very good idea," Daphne said. "As soon as she leaves, we'll go in and find Caspian."

"I'll have to be the one who goes in," JenniFur said. "And then I'll come out and tell you where he is, Nell."

I relayed to the others what JenniFur had said. "I wish we could go tonight," I lamented. "I don't like the thought of Caspian staying there another night, in mortal danger. Who knows what's happening to him!"

"I'd like to rescue him tonight as well," Edison said. "But Nell, we have to make this a successful rescue. We can't make a half-baked effort. If we go tomorrow, when Nora is away from her house, we have a very good chance of rescuing him. If we go tonight, she could use Old Magic on us. It could all end very badly."

"I know you're right," I said with a sigh. I was at my wits' end.

"Let's make our plan now," Edison said. "Then tomorrow, we'll be all ready to go."

Daphne tapped her chin. "We should wait down the road in a car."

"But she will see us when she drives past," Delilah protested.

"Obviously, we will park down a side street near another car, so she won't see us," Daphne said. "As soon as she drives past, we can go to her house. We'll let JenniFur out to find Caspian and see what's going on. As soon as JenniFur reports back to Nell, we'll all go in."

"Wait," I said.

They all turned to look at me.

"There must be a way to break the Concealment. Otherwise, will Caspian stay invisible forever?"

Edison looked as though he were trying not to laugh. "There is no way to break the Concealment, but the Concealment can only be applied to a small area. Once Caspian is out of the house, everybody will be able to see him. Hopefully, he will know where the book is as well."

"I want to help," Harriet said.

Daphne shook her head. "No, it's too dangerous."

"But I want to help!"

"Why don't I order pizza?" I said. "We'll all think better with pizza."

My ruse did not work. "I want to help!" Harriet said again. This time, she seemed far more distressed.

"I thought of a way you can help," I said. "We'll take two cars. Edison, you take your car and park on the main road to town. I'll take Daphne and Delilah in my car, and then collect you after you park your car. Harriet, you stay in

Edison's car, and if you see Nora Beckett's car coming back, call us at once, and warn us."

"Oh yes, that would be most necessary," Delilah said. "We will need an early warning system, that's for sure."

Harriet looked quite pleased but then said, "But I don't know what this Nora person looks like! And I don't know what her car looks like either."

"We'll take a photo of her car when she goes past," Delilah said.

Daphne disagreed. "That's a silly idea. We won't have much time to take a photo, and what if it's a bad one?"

"I saw her car in her driveway when I went to question her," I said. "It's a bright yellow Audi. She must have had it specially spray-painted, because they don't come naturally in that colour. Not as far as I know, anyway," I added as an afterthought.

I pulled up a photo on my phone of the same model Audi and showed Harriet.

"Oh yes, I know what those cars are!"

"I've seen that car around town, but I didn't know who owned it," Edison said.

Daphne and Delilah murmured agreement.

"Is that the only one in town?" Harriet asked.

"Oh yes, it certainly is," I said. "As I said, she must've had it specially spray-painted."

"So, do we have our plan set?" Daphne asked everybody.

We all nodded. "But what about the time?" I asked them.

"I know Nora often started cleaning Emerson's house at eight-thirty in the morning," Edison told us. "Why don't we leave here just after eight? That will give us time to set up."

"But what if she doesn't leave her house for a few hours?" Harriet said. "I'll be horribly bored."

"We will have to take that risk. After all, we're saving your uncle," I pointed out.

Harriet nodded but didn't look at all pleased.

"Then let's order pizza now," I said. "We'll all need to be fed and rested so we can carry out our plan in the morning."

That night, I didn't get to sleep until the early hours of the morning. I tossed and turned all night. JenniFur's words haunted me, that Caspian might have been in the room when I was there, and I had been unable to see him or hear him. It was all too much.

My alarm went off at seven. I felt as though I

hadn't had a wink of sleep, although I would have had a few hours.

I showered and then went downstairs to the kitchen. "Feed me," JenniFur said.

I put some food into her bowl and then stood there, waiting for her to ask for it again. It only took a minute or two.

"Feed me, I'm starving. I haven't eaten for hours," JenniFur said.

I poured the second packet of cat food into her bowl. "I'm cold," she said.

"It's not that cold."

JenniFur fluffed up her tail. "Cats feel the cold. We like to sit in front of fires. I need to be at my best so I can rescue your boyfriend."

"He's not my boyfriend."

JenniFur made a strange sound. I thought she was coughing up a furball, but then I realised she was laughing.

I rolled my eyes and hurried to the fireplace. The ashes from the night before were still smouldering. I threw some fire starter cubes on top of the ashes, scrunched up some newspaper around them, threw on some kindling and then a bigger log, and lit the newspaper, all in quick succession.

"There," I said to JenniFur. "And not another word out of you until I've had my coffee."

Thankfully, she stayed by the fire. I sipped my coffee slowly. Could this be the end of the ordeal? In a few hours, would we have Caspian back safely?

To my surprise, Harriet appeared. "You're up early," I said.

She simply grunted and fetched herself a bowl of cereal. "Where's JenniFur?" she asked. "She slept on my feet all night, and if I moved, she scratched me."

"She's by the fire," I said. "She's looking forward to being a hero."

"Don't you mean heroine?"

I shrugged.

Harriet pushed on. "Do you really think we will find Uncle Caspian this morning and rescue him?"

"I certainly hope so. That's the plan, anyway."

Soon, Edison arrived with Daphne and Delilah, and they had brought croissants. We feasted on croissants and drank coffee, but the mood was sombre. I was nervous that Nora might try to murder us all with Old Magic, but my concern for Caspian spurred me on.

"Just think, in a few hours we might have the book," Edison said.

"And Caspian." I shot him a glare.

He had the grace to look embarrassed. "Oh yes, of course. And Detective Cole too."

The next hour passed quickly. Before I knew it, I was in my car with JenniFur, Daphne, and Delilah. I drove towards Nora Beckett's house, with Edison driving behind me. "Keep an eye out for Nora's car in case she's making an early start," Daphne said.

We had looked at maps the previous night over pizza and had decided where we would park the cars. I pulled over at the spot where Edison was going to park his car. He parked his car and got out, leaving Harriet in the car.

"She has her phone. I checked that it's fully charged," he said.

"Excellent." As soon as Edison was in the car, I continued on. My heart was beating out of my chest. I parked in the appointed spot. "JenniFur, keep down. If Nora sees a cat in the car with us, she might get suspicious."

"On second thoughts we should all duck when she drives past," Delilah said.

"No, I have tinted windows," I said, as we drove down a side road.

"Then why did you ask me to stay out of sight?" JenniFur said.

I tapped myself on the side of the head. "Silly me! I'm just nervous, that's all."

Eight-thirty came and went. So did nine. I kept looking at my phone, expecting Harriet to call at any time to complain. I was wondering whether I should call her and ask how she was doing, when a yellow Audi appeared.

"It's her!" Daphne shrieked.

"I'll call Harriet." I called, and Harriet picked up at once. Before she could speak, I said, "Nora has just gone past us in the yellow Audi. She'll be going past you any minute. Call us as soon as she goes past you, and then call us immediately if she heads back this way."

"Honestly, Nell, I know the plan. I'm not a child," Harriet said. With that, she hung up.

A minute or so later, she called back. "She's just gone past me, heading into town."

"Thanks." I turned on the engine and drove down the road, parking a few houses away from Nora's but on the same side of the road. I opened the car door for JenniFur. "Here's your chance, JenniFur. Good luck!"

JenniFur ran towards Nora's house.

"What if Caspian isn't there?" I said.

"Everything points to Nora being a Concealer, so she must have been hiding something from you that day," Edison said

I nodded. My stomach clenched so much, it hurt. It seemed like an age before JenniFur returned.

I opened the car door, and she hopped in. "You won't believe it!" she screeched.

CHAPTER 23

"*W*hat is it?" I asked urgently.

"It's Caspian!" JenniFur said. "He's all right! She's got him chained in a bedroom."

"I brought bolt cutters just in case," Edison said.

JenniFur pushed on. "I mean, he doesn't look a picture of health or anything, but he's not dead. That's got to be a plus." She hesitated for a moment and then added, "He doesn't look at all well, but he's alive. After a few cans of salmon, I'm sure he'll be good."

"Did you see the book?" Edison asked.

"Oh yes, the book. It's on a desk in the bedroom."

"Okay, let's go in and fetch him." I was already halfway out of the car.

JenniFur and I hurried in front of the others. "Oh, the door is locked," I said with dismay. "JenniFur, how did you get in? I didn't even think to ask you."

"That window there is open wide," JenniFur said.

I went over to look at it. To me, it looked like a locked window.

"It must be part of the Concealment," Edison said.

I put my hand out and felt glass. While I did so, JenniFur climbed through it, so I pushed against the glass with my hand. To my surprise, my hand passed through. "It isn't glass. It's all in your mind," I said.

I dived headfirst through the window. At least, that was my intention, but my bottom got stuck.

"I'll shove you in," Daphne said. She shoved a little too hard. I landed with a thud and said some rather rude words.

"Through here," JenniFur said. "You'll have to open that door."

"How did you get in there?" I asked JenniFur.

"There was another window open around the back," she said. "What are you waiting for?"

I opened the door. "I can't see anything," I said to JenniFur.

"He is right in front of you. You'll have to explain to him what's happening."

"Caspian!" I yelled. "We can't see you because Nora Beckett is a Concealer. Yes, I know they aren't supposed to exist these days, but she's one for sure. I can't see you or hear you. Concealment doesn't work on cat Seelies, so JenniFur is going to guide us. By the way, Harriet is fine. She's been staying with me."

"He's not deaf," JenniFur said. "He can see and hear you."

I ignored that remark. "JenniFur, quick, Edison needs to use bolt cutters to cut the chains off Caspian. You'll have to guide him. Tell me, and I'll tell Edison."

"Caspian is five paces ahead of you," JenniFur said.

"Edison, JenniFur says Caspian is five paces ahead of you."

Edison let out a yell. "Ouch!"

"I might have misjudged the number of

paces," JenniFur said. "Still, it's good that Edison knows where Caspian is."

"I can feel him!" Edison said with excitement. "JenniFur, is it safe to cut here?"

I relayed his question to JenniFur. "And make sure it's perfectly safe before you answer," I said. "We don't want him cutting off any fingers."

"Yes, that's just a bit of chain. You'll have to cut it in two places. Caspian's hands are chained together, and then there's a very heavy chain linking him to the wall," JenniFur said. "Edison is close to the chain between Caspian's hands, but the chain to the wall was much thicker."

Once more, I relayed JenniFur's words.

Soon, JenniFur told us that Caspian was free. "I'll grab him, and we'll get out of here," Edison said.

We charged out of the room. We were halfway to the front door when I realised that Daphne and Delilah weren't there.

"Whatever happened to Daphne and Delilah?" I said to Edison as I flung open the door.

Standing there, on the front porch, were Daphne and Delilah. Nora Beckett was standing behind them, holding a gun.

I wondered why Harriet hadn't alerted us, but then I looked past Nora and saw a different car in the driveway. Emblazoned on the side of the car were the words, *Wild Lime Mountain Mechanics Courtesy Car*. Of all things! Nora had clearly taken her car for a service and was driving the courtesy car.

Nora shoved Daphne and Delilah into the room and stepped inside, locking the door behind her.

All at once, I could see Caspian. In fact, I could see everything. It wasn't an old, tired living room, after all. The furniture was luxurious, and a Hermes handbag was sitting on the coffee table.

"The Concealment takes energy," Nora said. "I'm glad you're all here and have revealed yourself as his friends. And here I was, thinking the detective didn't have any friends! Now I can torture you all to make him translate the book." She waved the gun at us and added, "You didn't think this through, did you?"

"What do you mean?" Edison asked her.

"Even if you had managed to rescue your friend here, how did you expect to apprehend me? Nobody can catch a Concealer. We're untouchable!" She laughed, a nasty, gloating laugh.

"Quick, Nell, do something," JenniFur said from under the sofa. "You're not in her register."

"I don't understand," I said.

Nora stared at me, clearly thinking I was addressing her. "Are you an idiot?" she said.

"How did you know Detective Cole was a Polyglot?" Edison asked.

"We're compiling a register of Seelie powers. I moved to Wild Lime Mountain ages ago and took a job as a cleaning lady so I could snoop. Nobody can catch a Concealer, and I'm a Concealer. How did you expect to apprehend me?"

I felt a hot flash coming on. Lately, I had discovered that hot flashes were, in fact, power surges. I shut my eyes and focused my energy. "Like this," I said. "You obviously didn't get too far with your register. I'm a Bookmarker."

Nora's mouth opened in shock. The next thing I knew, she uttered an ungodly scream. The room shimmered, and all at once, Nora was in the book, the ancient book of old magic.

"I hope she can't use Old Magic to escape from that book," JenniFur said.

"Edison, is Nora safely stuck in that book?" I asked him.

I think he answered in the affirmative, but I wasn't listening any longer.

Caspian pulled me to him. I wrapped my arms around his neck, half laughing, half crying.

After a moment, I stepped back, gazing up into Caspian's eyes. He had a bruised nose, which was sort of charming in a rugged way, and a graze across his forehead.

"You need to go to the hospital," I said.

Caspian shushed me with a wave of his hand. "I'm fine."

Panic rose within me. What if he had some sort of head injury? Head injuries were not the sort of trauma that should be taken lightly. I took a deep breath. "I can call an ambulance," I said. "Or I can drive you to the hospital."

Caspian exhaled deeply. "Nell, I'm not going to a doctor. I'm fine."

"At least let me take you to the nurse's office. We can go to the local school."

"What am I," Caspian said. "Thirteen?"

"Come on, Caspian. You could be seriously hurt."

"I need to call Sam Stevens and report Nora."

I was perplexed. "But what will you say to him? And where will you say she is?"

Caspian shrugged. "I have to say something, Nell. Something to explain my absence. I'll say that she abducted me and chained me up. I'll tell him I don't know why."

Delilah pushed me out of the way. "Call the other detective later, after the two of you have had some alone time." She shone her torch into Caspian's eyes.

I looked over her shoulder. His pupils dilated, which I figured was a good sign.

"Let's test your reflexes," Delilah continued. She punched Caspian in the knee.

"Ouch!"

"You seem fine," she said. "Just a little sassy."

Caspian sighed. "Can we go now?"

Delilah nodded. "Sure. Edison can drive, and we'll take you both to the botanical gardens. You can call us when you want to be collected."

Caspian agreed. "I don't want to call Stevens yet," he admitted. "I want a moment of peace and quiet—with Nell." His hand wrapped around mine.

At the botanical gardens, Caspian took my hand and led me to a pavilion. It smelt funny, like wood and moss, but not unpleasant. It smelt like a secret garden from a children's novel. In fact, the entire mountain smelt this way, strange and mysterious and pleasant, and I felt a surge of happiness.

"Are you okay?" Caspian asked. "I haven't had the chance to ask."

He continued to hold my hand as we sat on a wooden bench.

"I'm better than okay," I said.

"You're okay-er."

"Okay-er," I replied with a laugh. "No. I'm the okay-er-est."

"You know what's crazy?" Caspian said.

"What?"

He smiled at me, his eyes flashing with warmth and joy. "Despite everything that happened to me, with you here now, I'm the okay-er-est too."

And then we kissed.

$\mathcal{I}$ didn't know how to play tennis. I'd wanted to learn because everyone I knew loved tennis and because I loved tennis dresses, but my ex-husband had told me I looked like mutton dressed as lamb. Besides, he said, I didn't have the talent needed for such a sport. One night, he set his racquet and his gym bag on the table, and he told me that he would be giving lessons to our friend, Giselle, and that I wasn't to complain.

"Can't you give me tennis lessons?" I'd asked, confused.

"Don't be stupid," he had replied, and then he had left.

"You look adorable," Detective Caspian Cole

said, as he gently patted his tennis racquet on my back. "Earth to Nell. Are you ready to play?"

I exhaled sharply. I felt my face burn with shame. Harriet had talked me into buying a tennis dress, the kind of tennis dress that made mutton look like lamb, and everyone could see me. Daphne, Delilah, Edison, Harriet, and Caspian. Even JenniFur, who was perched in the umpire's chair, looked down at me with confusion, or so I thought.

"I need to go home," I sputtered. The racquet felt slippery in my hand.

"But I'm teaching you tennis," Harriet protested. For some reason I didn't quite understand, Harriet needed to practise her tennis so the girls at school would think she was amazing. "You promised."

"You don't know how to play tennis," I said. I sensed anxiety rising in my throat. "None of us know how to play tennis."

"I'm very good at tennis," Caspian said defensively.

"You asked where home base was," Delilah said.

"Is there no home base in tennis?" Caspian looked confused.

"Can I murder him?" JenniFur said to me, only everyone else just heard meows.

"You can't murder anyone," I retorted without thinking.

Delilah looked at me as though I was crazy. "I don't want to murder Detective Cole!"

I wiped my brow with the back of my hand. "Can't we just go on a picnic? I love picnics. We can have lemonade and read each other passages from our favourite books. Doesn't a picnic sound nice?"

The tennis court belonged to a grand old estate on Wild Lime Mountain. People could rent the court from the owners as there were no public courts in the town.

"No one is allowed in the house," Carla Pembroke, the owner, had said when we arrived. I soon discovered she was a thoroughly mean woman. "We don't have a servants' entrance anymore, and I don't like your sort entering from the front. The Pendragons might see and think we're entertaining a certain sort of guest."

"What sort of guest would that be, ma'am?" Caspian had asked innocently.

She jabbed a finger at him. "You know exactly what sort."

Harriet jutted out her chin. "It's rude to treat people like that."

"I'm not treating you, you *people* like anything," Carla sneered. "Maybe you are imagining things." With that, she stormed off.

"I'm glad she's gone," Harriet said. "I used Uncle Caspian's credit card and hired us a tennis coach."

Before Caspian could ask Harriet what she meant, the tennis coach ran in our direction, carrying a large tennis bag. He was a short, stout man who wore a red tracksuit and a matching red sweatband across his forehead.

He would have run past us if Harriet hadn't caught him by the elbow. "Are you here to teach us tennis?" she asked.

The man hesitated for a moment. "Obviously," he replied.

He did not say hello, because he told us greetings were for the weak, and he made us all line up and do push ups. I did not believe in push ups because I stood against everything push ups stood for, but the short tennis man was terrifying. Even Caspian seemed on edge.

"Now," the tennis coach said, "we play chess."

He did not offer us his name, and he did not

offer us any explanation as to why he was teaching us chess and not tennis. Evidently, this was how he coached all his pupils, because he had a chess set ready to go in the back seat of his car, which was a Mustang and smelled like leather and sandalwood.

"Stop looking at him," Caspian hissed in my ear.

"I'm not looking at him." I chuckled at Caspian's display of jealousy. Maybe I didn't look like mutton, after all.

We were all gathered around the tennis coach and Daphne, who were currently playing chess. Here is the thing about chess: I knew less about chess than I did tennis. I stopped feeling anxious and started to feel a little irritated. I was here in this stupid dress and in this stupid heat, and I wanted to be at home in bed watching television and eating chocolate.

"You can't take your eyes off him," Caspian said, his eyes flashing. "Do you find him attractive?"

"No," I lied. I don't know if I'd been in the wilderness since my husband's affair, but the tennis coach was maybe a little bit attractive? I didn't like men who were shorter than I was, but there was something about his intensity that was a little attractive, truth be told.

"Nell," the tennis coach barked. "You're next."

"But I don't know how to play chess."

The tennis coach flipped the chess board over, scattering the pieces. "Chess is over. Now—now we play tennis."

"I don't know how to play that either!" I cried softly.

"No matter," he said.

I watched with amazement as the tennis coach did all the things with a tennis racquet I could not do—like hold it correctly, for one. Then I listened with amazement as the tennis coach patiently talked to me about tennis. This was no ex-husband having an affair with Giselle, and this was no ex-husband who found me ridiculous. In fact, he seemed to find me quite cute. Of course, I only had eyes for Caspian, but I couldn't deny I was enjoying the attention.

"Do we play now?" I asked after half an hour.

"No, oh, no," the tennis coach replied. "First, we must become one with the tennis."

Becoming one with the tennis seemed to mean sitting cross legged on the court as we all closed our eyes and hummed. I didn't know the first thing about tennis, but I didn't think learning how to play involved chess and meditation.

"And we are done for today," the tennis coach said. "Nell, carry my chess set to the car."

We were all too stunned to speak. It took us about ten minutes to find the chess pieces, which were scattered all around the court. JenniFur had nibbled on one of the pawns, and it was all chipped with teeth marks.

I carried the set to the Mustang and helped the coach put it in his car.

"You are excellent at tennis for a beginner with no natural ability," he told me.

"Er—thank you?" I stammered. It was a strange day.

"I will never forget you," he said, and he jumped into the Mustang, rolling down his window.

The tennis coach reached through the window and kissed me, just once, just briefly, on the back of my hand. "I would tell you my name, but a man is entitled to his secrets," he said, and with that, he drove away in his Mustang, never to be seen again.

Caspian appeared at my elbow, frowning. "You are such a flirt," he muttered.

"I didn't flirt once," I replied, blushing.

Caspian drew me to him and kissed the top of my head.

We returned to the court, Caspian with his arm around my shoulders. Everyone was lying in the sun, overheated but happy.

"I liked that coach," Harriet said. "He was intense but in a super cool way."

I nodded. Daphne and Delilah left and returned ten minutes later with a picnic. Pink lemonade, cucumber sandwiches, cheese and biscuits. We ate happily, and we ate in silence, and we ate knowing that, at least for now, we were all safe.

"Is Harriet here?" A man entered the tennis court. "My name's Jim. Sorry I'm late. Car trouble."

"Jim?" Harriet said.

"The tennis coach. You hired me to teach your Uncle Caspian and a couple more people tennis."

"But if you're the tennis coach," I said, "then who was that man?"

Edison started to laugh. Then Harriet joined

him. Soon, we were all cracking up, and even JenniFur purred loudly. Who was that strange man if not the tennis coach?

"Thief!" the woman of the manor shrieked. She ran out of the estate. "A thief broke in and tied me up with the straps of my Chanel handbags. It took me ages to get free without damaging them. He stole all my jewellery! He even stole my husband's red tracksuit and matching red sweatband! Did anyone see which way he went?"

"Nope," I said, and everyone backed me up. We were all lying, naturally. But Carla Pembroke had been awful to us, whereas the fake tennis coach but real thief had taught us chess and meditation, and even tennis. We were on his side.

"Maybe you are imagining things," I added.

I stretched back on the court, grinning, with Caspian beside me. Maybe I was mutton dressed as lamb, after all. Maybe that's what I liked.

ABOUT MORGANA BEST

USA Today Bestselling author Morgana Best survived a childhood of deadly spiders and venomous snakes in the Australian outback. Morgana Best writes cozy mysteries and enjoys thinking of delightful new ways to murder her victims.

www.morganabest.com

Made in the USA
Middletown, DE
08 August 2021